ABSORPTION
Vegas

ABSORPTION
Vegas

Created and **Written**

By

Brooklen Borne
&
Donna Michele Ramos

ABSORPTION
   Vegas (Book **One** of **Four**)

Published by Ramos Barrington Entertainment
Sacramento, California and Irving, Texas

The cataloging-in-publication data is on file with the Library of Congress.

Library of Congress Control Number 2013934575

ISBN 13: 978-0692332733
ISBN 10: 0692332731

Printed in the United States of America
November 2014

Cover by: Jewelness
Edited by: Lena V. Anderson
Genre: Fiction/Crime/Thriller/Drama

Dedication

Donna Michele Ramos: My portion of the book is dedicated to my two children, my son Kyshaune and my daughter Keyonna. You have brought me much joy and I am proud to be your mother. Love you both.

Brooklen Borne: I would like to dedicate this book to my Editor Lena V. Anderson, In Memoriam, Frank K. Barrington, Mary Ann Hasan and all the current and future readers of this book and the rest of the ABSORPTION series. One Love!

Acknowledgements

To all of the wonderful, supportive book readers, who have purchased this book; we deeply appreciate you and look forward to bringing you more great reads.

Brooklen Borne & **Donna Michele Ramos**

The Authors' Other Books

Books by **Donna Ramos**

High Rise
Borrowed Time
Scandalous
Hawaii Three-O
DEAR DIARY…Not Quite (Children's Book)

Books by **Brooklen Borne**

The Write Lover
Savannah
The Interrogators
KAT
Any Given City

Chapter One
Senator Davis

A man who seems to be very upset is pacing back and forth in the kitchen of his ranch style home. "Do they really think they are going to do this to us and it's going to be alright? All those involved, plus some others, will pay the ultimate price for their bullshit red tape," he said out loud to an empty house as he continued pacing back and forth. He suddenly stopped pacing and sat down at the kitchen table. Tapping his fingers with the facial expression of a person in deep thought, his expression changed like a great idea had just popped into his head. He got up and went to the pantry to grab a family-size bag of plain potato chips, then goes to the refrigerator and retrieves a bottle of soda; before heading down the stairs to the basement.

*****

Using his background in physics, the disgruntled man stood at a table in the middle of a well-lit basement. Meticulously, he put together ingredients that will do something to the body that is so bizarre, there is not a special effects person in the movie industry that could compare. He tested this process many times on rats, dogs, cats, birds, and lizards and was successful each time. He then designed a dissolvable casing that would house the special ingredient in bullet form.

Once the deadly bullets were made he placed them in a small container, before putting them in the deep freezer that was located in the corner of the basement. The soon-to-be serial killer walked across the room and opened a newspaper that was lying on the table. He picked it up and flicked through a couple of pages, until he came upon a picture of California State Senator Davis, accompanied by statements about budget cuts. "This guy doesn't think he can be touched", the man said to himself.

*****

Exactly one week from the date of making the first set of bullets, the upset man was about to carry out a shooting that would produce fear on a scale never known to the human race. With a cold heart, and eyes filled with deep hatred, this serial killer in the making is about to see if his special bullets of death will do the damage they are intended to do. Looking through the scope that was attached to the rifle, the man focused on Senator Davis as he approaches the podium to give his speech. He placed the crosshairs on the senator's left shoulder. With his right index finger, he slowly pulled the trigger back; launching the liquid filled bullet to its target. A few seconds later, the senator yelled out in pain, grabbing a hold of his shoulder as blood trickled through his fingers.

Absorption Vegas

"The senator has been shot!" Someone in attendance screamed out. As security rushed to the senator's aid, a black limousine came to a screeching halt ten feet from where the senator was laying. Security shoved the senator into the limo, speeding away with a police escort to the nearest hospital. In the meantime, part of the security detail, and other law enforcement agencies, frantically search the area trying to locate the shooter. The senator was rushed straight to the operating room upon arrival.

"Get me some x-rays stat!" The chief surgeon barks, not breaking stride as they continued toward the operating room.

Once in the operating room, the senator was being prepped when a nurse walks up to the chief surgeon with x-rays in hand and said, "Doctor, the x-rays aren't showing any bullets."

"What do you mean?"

"The x-rays aren't showing a bullet. There's no bullet inside of the senator's shoulder." They momentarily looked at each other, then back at the x-rays with a puzzled expression.

"Okay, let's treat him for this phantom gunshot wound," the chief surgeon replied.

*****

"Welcome to WHDB News 11 at noon. I'm Sandra Kirkpatrick."

Borne & Ramos

"And I'm Marcy Alexander. Today's big story is the shooting of Senator Davis a week ago, as he gave a speech at the Ritz Carlton, in downtown Los Angeles."

The studio showed the viewer's footage of the senator getting shot during his speech. After the footage the co-anchor went on to say, "We have a crew on the scene. Nala White is at Mercy Hospital, where the senator is about to hold a press conference. Nala, what's going on? It looks like security is super tight."

"Good afternoon Nancy and Sandra. Security here today is very tight. Just a week ago Senator Davis was shot in the shoulder by an unidentified gunman. Police say the shooter is still on the loose. The chief surgeon said when they took x-rays to locate the bullet, there were none and no sign of an exit wound. He also said whatever the senator was shot with didn't cause any damage to any major arteries, it only tore through flesh and muscle. The chief surgeon also said, 'It's a mystery to us all what happened to that bullet.' It's also remarkable that Senator Davis is holding a press conference today. He just walked up to the podium. Stand by," the reporter said, relaying all available information to the studio and the viewing audience.

"Good afternoon everyone. I'm holding this press conference to let the American people, and my constituents, know that I'm fine but still recovering from an attempt on my life. This is a prime example of the need for the gun control bill that I'm working on getting passed. People are so quick to pick up a gun to shoot others that are unarmed. I call these types of people, punks. The media and their sources like to say these people have mental problems. Well, let me tell you…there are many people walking among us with mental issues and they are not out here shooting people. These people that shot me, and countless others, are nothing but cowards. I hope they catch him and take his freedom."

"Senator Davis, how could a gunman get close enough to shoot you and not get caught by the security detail that surrounds you?" A reporter from the BBC asked.

"I will let the Chief of Police elaborate on that a little more."

The Chief of Police stepped up to the microphone on the podium. "We looked at the surveillance cameras in the area, and it showed no one in the immediate area approaching the senator. The shot had to be from a sniper, a long distance away," he replied.

"This question is for the senator, senator what kind of bullet were you shot with that the doctors couldn't find it through x-rays or MRI's?" Another reporter asked. When Senator Davis leaned toward the microphone to respond, he collapsed as if he were falling apart. Some reporters gasped loudly; as a few others, along with security, rushed toward the senator. One female reporter screamed out, as the others stood in shock, from the horror their sight was projecting to their brains. Sounds of pictures being snapped, and voices, filled the room; while cameramen and soundmen were jockeying for the best position to film the senator's disfigured body. The senator had turned into a puddle of skin and muscle.   All the bones in his body had disintegrated.

Chapter Two
The L.A. Detective

Kehli Joyce, known as KJ, is a Los Angeles Police Detective. There is nothing average or ordinary about her. Her name isn't even spelled the way it normally is. She has the height of a WNBA player, face of an 'A List' Hollywood movie star, body of a porn star, and the intelligence of a Rhodes Scholar. But, she is also a little rough around the edges; not because she wants to be, but because she has to be. She's kind of hard on men because it's her only way to protect her heart.

KJ was on the force 6 years before making detective. She definitely put in her time in Patrol as a Neighborhood Police Officer. She had worked prostitution stings, posing as a hooker; walking the stroll on the strip snagging so many Johns she lost count. After seeing several narcotics undercover operations go south, she drew the line deciding to further her career by working on being promoted to detective. She favored homicide, solving murders and catching murderers; so she set her sights on achieving that. Anyone who knows KJ knows whatever she sets her sights on, she gets. Two years later, she got her gold shield. Her first 7 months she was paired with an old-timer who had one foot out the door. But, she'd tell anybody who asked, she learned more from him, and his vast experience, in 7 months than on her own on the street as a patrol cop. When Dwight retired, she was sad to lose him as a partner; but happy that after a 28 year career, he could go out on his own terms to live his dream of camping and fishing whenever he felt like it.

They had only been on the street an hour before a guy approached them. "Is this one of your CI's (confidential informants)?" KJ asks Ramon.

"No, I've never seen him before."

"I wonder what he wants," KJ said.

"We're about to find out," Ramon replied.

"Officers, can you help me?"

"We'll try. What's up?"

"I just bought this and I don't think its real crack cocaine. Can you test my pipe so I can be sure?"

"Sure," Ramon said pulling out his testing kit. After putting the residue in it, the liquid turns from clear to blue.

"I've got good news and bad news for you. It is crack and since it is yours, you're under arrest."

Driving back to the station, KJ does all she can not to die laughing. After charging him with possession of cocaine and drug paraphernalia, they transport him to jail and his bail is set at $2,500. Finally as they are leaving the jail KJ let out the biggest belly laugh ever.

"Ramon, are we in the Twilight Zone or some sort of alternate universe? Who does that? Who walks up to the cops, pipe in hand, and asks them to test their crack to see if it's real? I can't stop laughing, my stomach is killing me." Ramon is laughing hard also.

"He has to be one of the dumbest druggies around. No one is going to believe us. They're going to swear we made this up. In his own way maybe he was asking for help. What do you always tell me partner?"

"We don't catch the smart ones."

"Damn straight."

After lunch they hit the street again. Ramon saw someone he thought could be a person of interest in the Madden murder. He pulled over and they got out.

"What's the problem, officer?"

"Let's see some I.D."

"What did I do?"

"Where were you last Tuesday, Gerard?"

"Home."

"Can anyone corroborate that for you?"

"I um my um my cousin."

"Does this cousin have a name?" KJ pipes in.

"Sam Quinn."

"What's his number?"

"901-3333, look I didn't do anything." KJ dials the number and Sam says Gerard was with him on Tuesday.

"Ramon his story does check out."

"There's something about him. KJ, run this guy. I think we can violate him. He's on parole, so if he's doing anything illegal his parole is revoked and he goes back to jail." It turns out he had not done anything so they had to let him go.

"There's something about that guy. He's good for some bulletin I read, I know it. I just can't remember what."

"Maybe it will come to you before the end of watch."

"Yea...maybe," Ramon agreed while taking the cuffs off of the suspect and setting him free.

Later in the shift, KJ and Ramon respond to a robbery in progress. The victim tells them he was standing outside his car, while his 2 year old daughter was in the car in her car seat. Two suspects pulled up in a vehicle down the street from him. One suspect approached him on foot and got into the passenger side of the victim's car. Flashing a handgun, he demanded money and threatened to harm the baby.

The suspect ordered the victim to drive to a bank and withdraw money. The victim drove, with the suspect in his vehicle to the bank, while the baby was still sleeping in the car seat. The second suspect followed the victim in the suspects' vehicle. The victim withdrew money from the ATM as the suspect stood behind him. Both suspects left in their vehicle with the victim's money and ATM card. The first suspect was a male Hispanic, 19-23 years of age, 6'1, 150-170 pounds, short black spikey hair; and dark grey hoodie and black pants. He was described as having a round face and buck teeth; and was armed with a handgun. The second suspect was a male white, dark hair, height unknown; since he was seated in the car. The suspects' vehicle was a black 1990 2 door Chevrolet Nova, or Cavalier; partial license plate: 374 G. The suspect pointed in the direction the car took off in, north on Broadway.

Absorption Vegas

Ramon says, "They have a 6 minute head start on us. We need to get it in gear KJ." She drove while Ramon entered all the available information the victim gave them into the MDT (Mobile Data Terminal), hoping to get a hit on the partial license plate. The car wasn't very common so they may get lucky. "KJ, I got a hit on the plate, 374 GTE. Looks like it will work."

"What's the address?" KJ asked while speeding down block after block.

"5744 Stoneman Blvd," Ramon answered back while clicking on his seatbelt.

"We're only 5 blocks away from there. This is looking good."

They pulled up behind the car and one suspect was sitting in the car. They approached him and he instantly began to resist arrest. After fighting with him, they finally get him down. KJ had just finished cuffing the first suspect, when suddenly the second suspect jumped out of nowhere; lunging at KJ. Her back was to him, but she sensed someone behind her. Before she could turn around, Ramon punched the second suspect in the face, bringing him down. She put the first suspect into the back of their car and walked back over to Ramon. She looked at him over the suspect; together they pulled the second suspect up to his feet. Ramon put him into the back of their car. They got into the car and drove downtown to the central jail. After signing off on their prisoners, KJ looked at him again.

"What?" he asked. "I know that look. You gave it to me when we were cuffing the suspect."

"Good work."

"What else?"

"Thanks... but you didn't have to do that, Ramon. I had it under control."

"I know you did, but that's why I'm here. That's what partners are for. I will always have your back, KJ."

"Yea, you do. I'm here for you, too."

"Great, you can show me just how much."

"What are you talking about? We don't get down like that."

"Potty brain, it's not my fault your mind immediately dove into the gutter. I was getting ready to say since you're so appreciative you can buy me dinner. Its past lunchtime and we never went Code 7 (got a chance to eat). We were too busy running down those ATM suspects."

"Hahaha, my bad. Sure partner, one dinner coming up." Forty-five minutes later as Code 7 is winding down Ramon says, "I have a funny story for you."

"You always say that and you are not funny. Dude, when are you going to make peace with it? You are not a comedian."

"This is really funny. Just hear me out."

"Alright, go ahead."

"So, the Dispatcher answers the phone '9-1-1'. The caller says, 'Yea, I'm having trouble breathing. I'm out of breath. I think I'm going to pass out.' The Dispatcher asks, 'Sir, where are you calling from?' The caller replies, 'At a pay phone on the corner of South and Main'. Dispatcher replies, 'Hold on sir, an ambulance is on the way. Are you asthmatic?' Caller answers, 'No.' Dispatcher asks. 'What were you doing before you started having trouble breathing?' Caller answers, 'Running from the cops.'

"Really, Ramon? Really? That was a dumb story."

"But it was true. It's an outtake from an actual 9-1-1 call log."

"We always say, we don't catch the smart ones," KJ added.

"We'd better get back to the station. LT's been on a tear lately," Ramon said.

"Yea, his panties are always in a bunch lately. I wonder what's eating him. Then again, with him ripping on everyone all the time, it's probably better I don't know."

The next morning, KJ overslept and just couldn't get herself going. She was almost an hour late. Her Lieutenant wasn't too pleased. She used her department issued cell phone and told Ramon to swing by the station and pick her up. Fifteen minutes later, they're driving to interview a possible witness.

"What's wrong with you? Do you have a death wish or something?" Ramon asks.

"Don't you start in on me, too. I already need a pillow to sit on, thanks to the LT chewing my butt off. That man is wrapped too tight. He's always on our case but I've never seen him this pissed off, at least not all the time."

"Yea, he definitely has something going on with him." Ramon looked at her long and hard. "You look like you need to fill a sink up with coffee and dunk your head in it."

"Damn partner, a lady loves to hear such sweet words. Why don't you just come out and say, damn girl you look bad."

"KJ, don't you start with me. I'm just saying you look like you had a tough night. Are you cool?"

"Yea. I couldn't fall asleep and then when I did, it was time to get up and I couldn't. When I did get up, I just couldn't get going."

"I know how that is. Let's get you the tallest cup of coffee we can find."

"Such sweet words, exactly what I wanted to hear. You've redeemed yourself," she told him. He chuckled as he pulled into Pete's Coffee House. Ramon went in and got their coffee while KJ sat in the car. She closed her eyes and put her head back on the headrest. "OMG, I could use another couple of hours of sleep," she said aloud.

Ramon came back too soon with the coffee. She could have taken a power nap if he'd taken longer. Maybe she should figure out how to get this coffee to go directly into her veins and have an I.V. drip going all day. It seemed like that was the only way she could get through the day. KJ hoped nothing major happened because she didn't feel like she had the strength to run after anyone, today. "Bad guy bonus day. I'm not running after anybody. They'll get away today for sure. Hope it doesn't come to that", she realized.

Thankfully, the day was uneventful. But, the next day started with a bang. Roll Call went fine. Their Lieutenant told them, "The Chief just advised me they are expecting significant disruptions to normal traffic flow in the downtown district tomorrow, starting around 1000 hours through 1800 hours. Obviously, this will impact the lunch rush and evening commute. These lawful and permitted protests are sponsored by immigration rights groups and the numbers are expected to swell to 10,000 plus. Traffic conditions will not be good. If you need to bring people into the station, only do it if it's necessary. If the interview can wait, bring them in the day after."

After roll call, the Lieutenant tears into everybody. "What in the hell is wrong with you guys? Can't you solve your cases quicker? What happened to cracking down on the gangs? What do you do out there in the streets all day?"

KJ was still in a bad mood from the day before; a lack of sleep will do that to you. Not really wanting to hear his rant she pipes up, "Lieutenant with all due respect, we are solving a greater percentage of homicides this year than last year. We have partnered with other agencies and that has given us more resources; and there is an ongoing crackdown on gangs. We've made arrests in 31 out of the 47 homicides, so far. This time last year, we had only cleared 30 of 62. That's almost a 20 percent increase in solving cases."

"Thank you, Det. Joyce, for the patrol statistics. But have you forgotten about the old cases that had no movement or arrests in the last year? I'm getting my butt chewed out by the Captain because he is getting his butt chewed out by the Chief; and the Chief is getting fed up with getting an earful from the Mayor. He's at the Mayor's office so much that his name should be on the Mayor's door too. Get your asses in gear and clear up these old cases. The media is breathing down the departments' back, on two high profile cases that have not had any movement in the last 7 months. Detective Joyce, in my office! Everyone else is dismissed." KJ got up, looked at Ramon, and walked into the office. Ramon went to get the car, gassed it up, and waited in back of the station for her. KJ took a seat in one of two chairs in front of the lieutenant's desk.

"You are on the verge of being written up for your punctuality because you are always late. Do you think criminals will stop committing crimes until you can make it into work? Hell no, they won't. You will be on the street when your shift begins or else you will pay with a suspension. And if you ever undermine me like that again, I'll bring you up on insubordination. You got that?" He bellowed.

"Affirmative," she replied, glaring at him.

"Dismissed!" He barked.

*****

"Thank God I'm off tomorrow. I will rip his head off if I have to look at him anymore this week," she told Ramon while getting into the car.

"KJ, why do you do that? Why do you insist on bumping heads with him? He's your boss!"

Absorption Vegas

"He pissed me off! We're busting our butts in the field while he's sitting on his fat ass in his air conditioned office, shuffling papers around. The only thing he does is go from meeting to meeting and he has the nerve to say we aren't doing anything."

"Point taken. But, do you have to antagonize him by calling him out in front of everyone?"

"The stuff he says is so infuriating."

"You're right, but can't you talk to him in private? It would go over better if your comments were just between you and him."

"I can't trust myself to be alone with him. I do carry a gun."

Ramon threw his head back and laughed, a big from-the-belly laugh. "You are certifiable, KJ."

"Yea, but you love me anyway."

"Yea, I do. You are the craziest partner ever; but you're my crazy partner."

"Damn straight! What do you think about this Homeland Security Defense Training Workshop we're mandated to attend next week?"

"I can't believe it. We never get to go to any kind of training because we aren't a specialized unit, and now we've got training two months in a row. I'm not dying to go but hell, its paid time off. I'm looking at it like 3 days away from the grind."

KJ thought for a minute, then looked at him, "You have a point. Yea, at least I'm away from the Lieutenant."

"There you go. Not as bad as it seemed at first, right?"

"No, now it's cool."

Toward the end of their shift Ramon says to her, "I've been thinking."

"It's always scary when you try that," KJ teased.

"How long have we been riding together?"

"Seven years," she answered.

"Seven years; I might need to get a new partner."

"You what?" Shocked, she asked.

"I think I have the seven year itch. I need to get someone less stable."

KJ cracked up laughing, "There's no one less stable than me. You had me there for a minute partner. I thought you were serious."

"No problem there, KJ. You're stuck with me too, like a bad marriage." They both howled with laughter.

Chapter Three
My Partner

Three months later, KJ's life seemed to have calmed down and she was doing really well with her punctuality. Guess things were going too good, because that morning her car wouldn't start; her battery was dead. There was no one around to get a boost from, so she had to wait for the auto club to come. Forty-five minutes later, she was finally on the road. Traffic was worse than usual, if that were possible. L.A. traffic had to be the worst in the world. Now, she was almost two hours late for work. "I have to get some coffee before I take another step. I'm already super late, so a few more minutes isn't going to make a difference", she thought to herself. After waiting in line for over ten minutes, she finally got her coffee and pulled off from the drive-thru window. Pulling into the parking garage, her coffee was finally cool enough to sip.

"Ugh! This is disgusting! How do you get black coffee from an order that's supposed to be coffee extra light, with 2 sugars?" She said, fussing at no one in particular. KJ's day could not possibly get any worse; boy was she mistaken.

"Hey. Good morning Sunshine," Ramon teased.

"Don't start with me. I'm not having a good day."

"I hadn't noticed."

"Don't be a wise ass, Nieves. I'm not in the mood."

"Okay, Dragon Queen, I get it," he quipped.

She went through the bulletins on her desk wondering when it was going to slow down. "We'll never get caught up. Cases coming in double digits before we can even solve the ones we already have. And they wonder why our old cases can't get solved. We don't have enough time to work on the new ones. How in the hell are we supposed to work on the old ones too?"

The sergeant came by with a bulletin. "You two take this and check it out."

"Yes sir," Ramon replied, getting up from his cubicle and walking over to KJ's.

"What's up?" she asked.

"We need to roll. We have to check this out."

"What did you agree to this time, Ramon?"

"What did I agree to? You make it sound like I had a choice to say, no. The sergeant ordered us to do this."

"Yea whatever partner," KJ said sarcastically.

An hour later. "So, that was a bust." Ramon said, letting out a deep breath.

"It sure was." KJ replied looking out the window. "Let's go grab a bite to eat."

"What, are you bored?"

"Yea, Ramon, I'm a girl that craves action. How do you not remember that?"

"I just had a senior moment."

"You're lucky you got me as a partner."

"Oh yea, KJ. I forgot for a minute how lucky I am. I'm always running interference for you with the Lt. Explain to me again, how lucky I am."

"Whatever, Ramon. You're no bargain either!" She quipped. They start back to the station in silence. Ten minutes later, Ramon finally speaks, "KJ, look at that vehicle ahead of us. Anything look wrong to you?"
She looked at it. "It does look suspicious. Let's check it out."

As soon as they were close enough to the vehicle to ask for license and registration, the car peeled out. Now in pursuit, they call it in and check the license plate on the MDT.

"It's 10851 (stolen), like I thought. Punch it, we can't lose them!" KJ added.

Four blocks later, they found the car abandoned. Ramon quickly parked as KJ called in, updating their location.

"We are now in a foot pursuit on the northwest corner of Sepulveda and LaCienega. Two suspects, one male Black, 30-40, black leather jacket, black beanie hat; the other a male Hispanic, 30-40, jeans, grey hoodie, bald head." Bounding out of the car, they start running after the suspects. Seeing them duck into the convenience store, KJ signals for Ramon to go to the back; motioning to him she'll cover the front. Before KJ could get into the front door, shots were fired. Cautiously, she entered, checking the security mirror to see if she could locate the shooter. Finally seeing him, she goes left to circle around to come up behind him. Another shot pierces the air, but it's not inside the store. She got the drop on the suspect, subduing and cuffing him. Running terrified to find out where the two shots outside ended up, she saw Ramon on the ground.

"Ramon! Ramon, get up!" she yelled. Searching his body, she saw his vest had stopped one bullet. But, the second one was leaving a nasty gash and blood trail from his right temple. Trying desperately to stem the flow of blood she entreated him, "Ramon, open your eyes. Look at me man!" His eyes slowly fluttered open.

"Hey partner," he replied weakly. "Sorry he got away."

"Do you think I give a damn about that? I need you to stay with me!"

"Trying, KJ. I'm trying." But his body went slack in her arms.

"Ramon, the ambulance is coming. I know you can hear it. Hang on, partner! Hang on, please!" She pleaded with him.

Ramon was now unconscious. The paramedics and backup finally arrived. They had to pry KJ away from him.

"KJ, move! The paramedics have to work on him." She turned to look at them. She didn't comprehend what they were saying. "KJ, now!" Her sergeant yelled.

Loathe to let go of Ramon, she whispered to him, "I'm sorry partner. I'm sorry I wasn't here." She was pushed to the side as the paramedics fought valiantly to stabilize him. When he was stabilized as much as possible, he was transported to the medical center. Within an hour, the waiting room was a sea of blue. Everyone was there to lend support, give blood, and pray. KJ was silent and withdrawn. In her mind, this was all her fault and he was dying because of her. Going over it in her mind, she'd let him down. She was not there and he was always there for her!

Two hours later, the doctor came out of emergency surgery. The prognosis wasn't good. They stopped the bleeding, but Ramon had lost so much blood; and the bullet had ripped through his frontal lobe.

The surgeon explained, "A frontal lobe is your brain's largest lobe. It controls your motor skills, like hand/eye coordination, conscious thoughts, emotions, and even your personality. Frontal lobe damage may impair your attention span, motivation, judgment, and organizational capacity."

"Your frontal lobe consists of a right and left lobe, or hemisphere. It's the hub of who you are; your emotions and personality. Both lobes deal with social, emotional, motor, and sexual behavior; as well as problem solving, decision making, and memory. Your left frontal lobe deals with language ability (the logical thinker); while the right frontal lobe is generally more concerned with non-verbal aspects of communication, such as the awareness of emotions in one's facial expressions. The right lobe is also in charge of picking up auditory signs such as the tone of voice when someone is angry, sad, or scared. The right frontal lobe is more involved with negative emotions, while the left frontal lobe is more involved in positive emotions. If he survives, there is no telling if he will be able to function enough to even take care of himself. I'm sorry I can't offer a better prognosis, but his condition is grave and you need to be prepared for the worst."

Ramon's sister Grace, also an officer, takes up vigil by his bedside. KJ knew she could go in, but the guilt was eating her alive. She had no right to go in there. She was too late. She should have been by his side when he was being ambushed.

It had been a brutal four days and Ramon had never regained consciousness. His advanced directive was clear, do not prolong his life artificially. There seemed to be no cerebral activity. Grace was at her wits end. She didn't want to lose her brother, but she didn't want to go against his wishes. Shortly after they both graduated from the academy, they talked about the quality of life they wanted if injured or shot on duty. Ramon emphatically stated he refused to be a pathetic vegetable or be hooked up to machines to prolong a life that he could not live.

KJ still couldn't bring herself to go back to the hospital. She couldn't eat or sleep. Grace called her after Ramon had a particularly rough night. She was almost hysterical. KJ realized she needed to go and help Grace, she should be there to support her. It was the least she could do. She had caused all this unimaginable grief and pain.

"Stop being selfish! Stop thinking of yourself and how you feel. Imagine how Grace feels watching her brother slip away from her," she chastised herself.

Two days later, while she was there with Grace, Ramon went into cardiac arrest. The doctors rushed in but didn't do anything. Grace screamed at them, "Help him! What are you waiting for?"

"Officer Nieves, I'm sorry but your brother's Advanced Directive states he does not want to be revived if something should happen to him."

The expression on Grace's face looked as if someone had just thrust a knife into her heart. "I can't do this, KJ. I can't sit here and watch my brother die!"

KJ got up and went over to hug Grace. "Grace you know how stubborn Ramon is. If he wants this, we have to follow his wishes."

"But I don't want to follow his wishes! I don't want him to leave me. What am I going to do if he leaves me?"

"Grace none of us want that. But we have to face facts and remember what he wants, and what the doctor said the last two times they ran that test on him. We have to face the possibility of him leaving us." Grace grabbed her brother's hand, weeping. She knew even though his breathing had gotten better, it wasn't good enough or strong enough; it was more of a reflex action. She knew with certainty, in his fragile state, he would not survive the night.

Tragically, she was right! End of watch for Detective Ramon L. Nieves was November 15, 2013, at 11:50 p.m.

Chapter Four
Stand Down Detective

Grace wanted KJ to ride with the family in the limousine, but KJ couldn't. The guilt of not saving Ramon still overwhelmed her. She felt she wasn't worthy of riding with the family because she believed his death was her fault. She could barely face Grace and Ramon's grandmother. There was no way she could ride with them. They didn't blame her for his death, but she did; every single day.

The funeral was held at First Congregational Church on Commonwealth Avenue, in Los Angeles. Police officers came from all over to say goodbye to another officer killed in the line of duty. There was a sea of blue, numbering in the hundreds, to pay their last respects to Officer Ramon Nieves. Thirty-seven different law enforcement agencies attended. Dozens of patrol cars and patrol motorcycles attended the funeral of their fallen brother. Officers from as far as New York and Hawaii attended, because no one appreciated the sacrifice Ramon made as much as his fellow officers who faced the same risk every day they suited up and hit the streets.

Borne & Ramos

The church was packed with law enforcement from various agencies, military personnel, people who had worked with him, and civilians that knew him well; along with a sprinkling of political dignitaries.

A beautiful silver casket, with gold trim and handles, was staged just below the pastor's podium. Being Ramon was also a former Marine, his casket was flanked by Marines; per request of the family. These guys look really sharp in their Dress Blue uniforms, KJ thought to herself as she looked around the church from where she was sitting. She sat with Ramon's family, next to his 90 year old grandmother, Elva. Everyone in Ramon's family adored KJ and thought they should get together, romantically. They used to tease both of them about hooking up because they looked so good together. They all thought they would make a wonderful couple. Even though at that time neither one was attached, they were afraid it would interfere with their working relationship.

KJ stared at the casket, reminiscing about her and Ramon's funny cases. A sad smile crept across her lips as the choir sang a couple of hymns. A few minutes later, the pastor stood up and walked up to the podium. When he began to speak, tears welled up in her eyes and overflowed down her cheeks. Ramon's grandmother reached over, taking KJ hands into hers.

"Baby, it's going to be alright. This is something we all have to face some day. We just don't know how it's going to happen."

"I know Grandma Elva," KJ replied, sniffling. "But the person that did this will pay."

After the recognition of attendees and various speeches, the casket was opened to take one last look at Ramon. He was dressed in a navy blue suit, light blue shirt, and navy blue tie. KJ lowered her head not wanting to see her partner and friend in that state.

Ushers came from the back of the church and posted themselves at every other pew. Starting from the front, an usher began directing family members, and those in attendance, toward the casket for the final viewing.

When KJ walked up to view his body, she could feel herself becoming light-headed and she felt like she was on the verge of passing out. It was taking every fiber of her being not to lose it.

She stared at Ramon, dressed out in the coffin. "Get up, please. You can't leave us. You can't leave me," KJ thought to herself. She leaned down and kissed him through tear filled eyes. "It's going to be hard to go on without you, Ramon," she said in a very low voice barely audible to those near her. As she slowly rose up, she realized the enormity of his absence from her daily life. The finality of never seeing him, or hearing his voice again, was too much for her to handle. Her legs gave away as her knees buckled. Her girlfriend, Diane, was standing behind her and caught her around the waist; stopping her from falling to the floor. A police officer saw what was happening and quickly ran toward them to assist Diane with KJ. Now fully supported, KJ was led back to where she was seated. KJ thanked him and the officer went back to his previous location.

A few minutes later, as the casket was being wheeled past her, KJ still couldn't believe this was really happening. But at the same time, she knew it was reality. Riding to the cemetery, she looked over at Diane. "This is a bad dream. I want to wake up, but I can't. He was my anchor. I feel like a boat that has been cut loose from the pier, drifting off into rough uncharted waters. Just being around him made me want to do better. We talked about everything and made each other laugh. Oh, how he could make me laugh. I love him so much." She leaned her head against the window, closing her eyes, as the tears flowed down her cheeks.

At the cemetery, the U.S. Marines and L.A.P.D. ceremonial details presented Ramon's grandmother with an American flag and California State flag, as a symbol of his faithful and dedicated service. The reason she was presented was because both of Ramon's parents were deceased.

The repast was held back at the church in one of the two halls that were on the church property. KJ showed up and sat with Elva and Grace for a little while, to make sure they were all right, before heading home. Diane dropped KJ off at home and told her if she needed anything that she better not hesitate to call. KJ thanked Diane and told her she just needed to be alone.

Back at her apartment, she came out of her clothes, throwing them about, as she walked toward the shower. As she began to bathe, the reality of Ramon's death hit her hard again. She cried uncontrollably as she slid down the wall onto the floor. The pounding water, mixed with her tears, traveled down the drain as she continued to scream out.

After a not so relaxing shower, KJ sat on the couch with the television on, but not really watching it. She leaned forward toward the coffee table, reaching for a half empty bottle of Ciroc vodka. Pouring a glass, she spilled some onto the table indicating her level of intoxication. She placed the glass to her lips and drank the contents as if it were water, before placing the glass down on the coffee table. Her cell chimed, startling her somewhat. She picked up the phone, knocking the empty glass to the floor. Trying to focus on the caller ID, she could make out it was her best female friend, Diane. KJ fumbled to answer it, but the phone fell to the floor. Not trying to retrieve it, she leaned back on the couch and passed out.

*****

A week and a half later, KJ was still wrestling with her demons and they had the upper hand. The only thing on her mind was getting those who killed Ramon.

"KJ, you need to distance yourself from this."

"Lieutenant, what are you talking about? I have to get that S.O.B. for what he did to Ramon."

"That's what I mean. We will get him, but you will stand down."

"Are you serious? I will not!"

At his incredulous look, she adds, "You can put me in for insubordination but I do not care. I will get this bastard for what he did and you will not stop me."

"You will take yourself somewhere for a few days until you calm down."

"I will not," she said coming out of her chair.

"SIT DOWN!" He barked. I know you're upset about your partner so I will not charge you with insubordination, yet. But if you do not get out of here and take at least seven days off, I will take your gun and badge, and personally escort you off the premises."

She looked at him in shock.

"When you come back from your seven day vacation, you will be riding a desk until the psychiatrist decides you are fit for duty. You will not pursue a personal vendetta on my watch. We are a unit and we will get that bastard together, no going off half-cocked. Are we clear, Detective Joyce?"

She wanted to tell him to go to hell. Actually, she wanted to tell him to go screw himself; but she answered, "Yes sir! Am I dismissed?"

The lieutenant looked at her long and hard, taking in her stance and the rest of her body language. She was pissed and looking to take it out on someone.

"The only thing you're gonna do is follow department regulations. You do know what department regulations are Detective Joyce, don't you? Before you leave for a week, you will go see Dr. Coxwell."

"The shrink? I thought you meant when I came back!"

"Whatever you want to name her, you will see the therapist. You will check in with her today before you leave. You will not be cleared for duty unless she clears you. Now, you are dismissed!"

Walking out of his office she mumbled to herself, "When I find that bastard, he will pray to be killed and I will gladly be his angel of death. I will send him straight to hell in the worst way possible." She fought the overwhelming urge to slam the door. It was like she could hear Ramon saying, "Cool it, KJ!" So, she closed the door behind her gently as the lieutenant looked at her through his blinds before walking over to close them.

*****

KJ pulled into the parking space in front of the fifteen story, modern mirrored building of her therapist. Shutting off her car and removing her seat belt, but not getting out, she took a deep breath and exhaled. "I really don't feel like I need this. The only therapy I need is to get back on the streets and crack a few heads to find the shooter who took my partner, and friend from me." She glanced down at her watch and reluctantly exited her car, walking toward the building.

She walked through the double glass doors and saw a directory on a nearby wall. Studying the directory, she saw the name Dr. Coxwell, 11 Floor, Suite A. Stepping off the elevator KJ noticed on the blue wall in front of her, in white lettering, the word 'Suite A' with an arrow,

Ramos & Borne

informing her she needed to go left. Walking down the hallway, she reached Dr. Coxwell's office. She paused momentarily, before turning the knob and entering. Dr. Sheila Coxwell was a no nonsense therapist. She was compassionate, but will tell you like it is and that it's up to the patient on how long it will take them to get back on the job. KJ walked into Dr. Coxwell's office for her mandatory meeting before leaving on her forced vacation.

"Hello Detective Joyce," Dr. Coxwell greeted with her hand extended.

"Hello," KJ replied, politely shaking her hand. She felt the last thing she needed was to be there, but didn't want to lose her job for not following departmental regulations.

"So what brings you here today?"

"C'mon doc, you know why I'm here."

"Detective Joyce, I know you are here because something happened on the job. I'm not here to play games or waste your time or mine. So I'll ask you again. What brings you to me, detective?" KJ sat in a chair across from Dr. Coxwell, not wanting to prolong her stay any longer than she had to; spoke with an attitude.

"My partner, and close friend of seven years, was murdered."

"How are you feeling about that?"

"About what?" KJ asked, looking at Dr. Coxwell in disbelief of the question.

"About the death of your partner."

"For real, doc! For real!" KJ responded, as she stood up and started walking toward the door.

"Detective Joyce, your session is not over. If you walk out of that door you will not be cleared for duty." KJ ignored her comment and continued walking, closing the door behind her. Walking hastily to her car. Once in the car, she closed her eyes and leaned her head back on the headrest, and thought to herself. *"Stupid bitch! How does she think I feel? I can't believe she asked me that idiotic question. Obviously seeing this shrink is going to be a waste of everyone's time."* She opened her eyes, putting the car in gear and speeding out of the parking lot.

Chapter Five
Sin City

"I will never get used to going to funerals. Never thought I'd be going to my partner's funeral. Maybe it's good I'm getting out of town for a few days. This four hour drive will do me good. I might be able to clear my head a little," KJ thought to herself.

Well into the four hour drive on I-15N toward Las Vegas, KJ kept going over everything about the day Ramon was killed. Should she have done this? What if she didn't do that? Was it her fault? Why him and not her?

After attending the Homeland Security Training with Ramon, KJ admitted to herself it had been more interesting than she would have thought. Now that Ramon was gone, she didn't want another partner. She really didn't want to be in that department without her best friend.

Everybody knows Homeland Security was made to prevent terrorism and enhance security. What she didn't know was that there was a Federal Protective Service Police (FPSP). FPSP provides integrated security and law enforcement services to federally owned and leased buildings, facilities, properties and other assets. It protects thousands of Federal facilities and safeguards millions of federal employees, contractors, and civilian visitors. FPSP provides super law enforcement and protective security services by leveraging intelligence and information from federal, state, local, tribal, territorial, and private sector partners.

Every day FPSP protects the homeland by managing risks and ensuring continuity for one of the most crucial elements of our national critical infrastructure – our nation's federal facilities and their occupants. KJ decided she would look into it a little more. It was definitely different from what she was used to doing and she kind of liked the idea of detecting, deterring, disrupting, and investigating threats using law enforcement authorities.

The last time KJ checked their pay scale, she found National Incident Management Assistance Team Leader III pay was $119K-$179K, with quicker upward mobility in the organization. The Feds pay was much better than LAPD.

Once again, everything reminded her of Ramon. Law enforcement was still in her blood, but she could stand a change. She could go to a different city or at least another law enforcement agency. She was seriously contemplating leaving LAPD and making a lateral move over to the Joint Task Force. Maybe a couple of years on loan to another agency will free her from her inner demons that refused to let go, since Ramon was murdered.

"The more I think about leaving this place, the more I'm starting to feel a complete change of scenery is what will

work best for me. As messed up as I am right now, it definitely couldn't hurt. But I feel like I am leaving my partner behind. He'd be the first one to tell me to go for it. Hell, he'd probably come with me." She smiled sadly, wondering when the gaping hole losing him had left in her heart would start to close. She knew it would never go away, but could she get a little peace; at least a little closure?

Checking her dashboard clock, she had made it to Vegas fifteen minutes ahead of the time she thought she would. Must be all the speeding in the desert, she thought. She pulled up to the semi-circle driveway. Glad to be out of the car for a while, KJ happily handed her keys to the valet, tipped him, and took her ticket from him. Another valet appeared and put her suitcases on a gold-toned metal cart and rolled away toward the lobby. Walking into the lobby of the Venetian, she was in awe of the beautiful structure of the place, and everything that was simultaneously going on around her. Getting checked in, she started chatting with the desk clerk. Before she knew it, her new buddy had given her an upgraded room on the seventeenth floor. Riding up in the elevator, the valet was sneaking peeks at KJ's figure. She caught him looking too long and he began to blush with embarrassment. She just smiled. Not wanting to interrupt his fantasy, she just turned her head to look at the numbers of the floors flash on the screen as the elevator passed by.

Once inside her room, the valet removed her luggage from the cart and asked if she needed anything else. She told him she didn't and tipped the young man before sending him on his way. As he closed the door, he had to take one last look at KJ's butt in her formfitting skinny jeans.

She walked over to the wall, pressed a button on a keypad, and the curtains began to open. There was a wall of glass, revealing a bird's eye view of the Vegas strip. Looking at the beautiful view, she thought about how much Diane would love it. KJ felt bad about not keeping in touch with her like she should have. But Diane was a good friend. The kind that didn't hold it against you if you didn't talk for months. KJ was blessed to have her in her life. If it wasn't for Diane, she didn't think she would have made it through Ramon's funeral or the past few weeks. She needed to call her and let her know that she was out of town and doing fine. This way, she would stop worrying so much about her.

That night as she ordered room service, KJ turned on the TV but didn't really pay attention to it. She started seriously thinking about either joining a Homeland Security Joint Task Force or even going to a new law enforcement agency altogether. "Maybe I should go on a ride-a-long, with the Las Vegas PD while I'm out here." she mumbled to herself aloud.

Since Ramon was killed on duty, everything reminded her of her failure to save him. She didn't have his back, but he always had hers. The bitter taste in her mouth refused to go away. After she finished eating she looked at the list of events in the hotel that week. Spying the literary conference, she decided to go when it started. Tomorrow she'd lay out by the pool.

"Real life sucks. It'll be nice to dive into a fantasy world, even if it's just for a few days. I can listen to the authors explain their thought process and how they created their characters. Then, I can figure out which characters I want to know more about and buy those books. Yea, poolside with a good book, some shade and a drink, sounds like that's exactly what my Lieutenant ordered. God forbid I'm actually agreeing with him on something," she thought, smirking to herself.

The next morning she went to the coffee shop and ordered a small coffee and a fruit salad. Book in hand, she headed to the gorgeous, column-trimmed pool. Finding the perfect spot, she dragged a chaise lounge over to it. She threw her towel on the chaise and gracefully laid down, carefully adjusting her new red bikini. Thirty minutes later, she was sipping a bloody Mary and reading her book. From time to time something caught her eye and she would stop reading to enjoy the eye candy that was in her view. It had been a minute since she had made love. She could use a bedroom workout session. "Love me hard, love me deep, wear me out, and put me to sleep." This was the song KJ would sing whenever she saw someone she'd like to make love to. "That guy is really hot," she said to herself when she saw Gino Bartolinni, the New York Times Best Selling Author, walk by. She had no idea who he was, only that he was hot!

Borne & Ramos

At first glance, people had mistaken Gino Bartolinni for the movie star, Dwayne Johnson; also known in the wrestling world as The Rock. He once was a stuntman and stood in for Dwayne as his double in a few movies. Gino had sustained a bad injury while filming a movie in Europe and was hospitalized for six months. With the abundance of down time during his healing process, he began writing stories. By the time he left the hospital, he had written two novels and a book of short stories. He managed to write another novel during his two months of rehabilitation after leaving the hospital. He now writes full time, getting paid more money than he ever did as a stuntman. The bonus for him is that he gets to stay in one place and enjoy his home. No more injuries, traveling from state to state, or country to country, for months at a time.

The next morning, KJ still had thoughts about Gino, the man she saw walk by at the pool. Not knowing his name, or why he was at the hotel, she just chalked it up as some eye candy that was there vacationing with his family. *"Let me get this man out my head,"* she thought to herself as she finished lotioning her body.

"Today's temperature is going to be in the triple digits, folks. If you don't have to go out, don't! But those of you that do, please stay hydrated. There have been reports of two heat related deaths due to the unusually high temperatures that are plaguing the western part of our nation." The weatherman on the local news station informed the viewers.

Absorption Vegas

"I guess that's my sign to keep my butt in this air conditioned building." KJ said out loud while gazing at her reflection in one of the many bathroom mirrors. She loved how good her new white jeans looked with her hot pink tank top. Realizing she needed to get out of her suite, she went downstairs and started roaming through the Grand Canal Shoppes. It was so ridiculously hot outside, even in the shade, that she opted on staying inside until it at least cooled down enough for humans to be outside. The 117 degree temperature, was not her idea of perfect weather to even lay by the pool. Hell, the pool probably feels more like bathwater in this ungodly heat. Maybe she could venture out to the pool this evening around 7 p.m. A cool 100 degrees would work, she chuckled to herself and thought only in Vegas can 100 degrees be considered cool.

With so much time to kill, and nothing to do, she decided to window shop and maybe do some real shopping too. It all depended on what she found. KJ lost her mind in Basin White. She couldn't help it. Everything she smelled, smelled better than the previous thing. She smelled so much stuff that her nose was in overdrive, after being so over stimulated. Though everything smells so divine, she'd spent so much time in the fragrance shop that she needed some fresh air. Quickly running outside, she breathed in enough air to clear her sinuses. The oppressive heat smacking her in the face sent her almost running back into the wonderful air-conditioned lobby and back to the Grand Canal Shoppes to continue her retail exploration therapy.

KJ went into 'Banana Republic', 'Cache', and 'BCBG'. She went into 'BEBE' and bought a top, silver sandals in Shooz, accessories in Vittorio; as well as a dress in Herve Leger. "I've got a really hot outfit here. Now, all I've got to figure out is where to wear it tonight. I can't believe I found this dress on the clearance rack and it's in my size. I was supposed to have this! It does fit like it was made for me."

In her now cleaned suite, thanks to housekeeping, KJ kicked off her shoes and laid across the bed. Picking up the remote control, she flicked through the channels until she came to the hotel's station. They were advertising an author's interview, in one of the three business halls in the hotel, for only $10.00 and tickets were still available. The tickets were cheap because the event was something new that the literary planners decided to add to their program and they wanted to see what kind of turnout they would have before making it a quarterly event.

"I'm going to this," she blurted out as she donned her red sundress, putting on her yellow accessories. Not caring which author was being interviewed, she just wanted to do something and possibly learn more about how an author thinks. She left the room and walked a short distance to the hotel's Business Center. She went online, purchased the ticket, and printed it out. Looking at the time on her phone, she had ten minutes to spare before the 'special guest' author did his interview in front of a live audience. Feeling a little thirsty, KJ walked over to the vending machine and reached inside her Coach Messenger purse to pull out two dollars. After inserting them into the machine, she pressed the plastic square button that released a 20 ounce bottle of Nestlé's Green Tea.

*****

KJ was walking toward the Hall when she saw him! Of all the people she had seen at the pool yesterday, who would have ever thought she'd see him here; as the main event. Hmmm, her luck seemed to be changing for the better. "I'll have to go and introduce myself to the object of my lustful thoughts," she said to herself, smiling predatorily as she continued to walk toward the hall.

She walked into the large, almost empty room and took a seat near the front of the stage. A few minutes had passed when the room began to fill up. Looking around the room, she thought about how she had gotten there in the nick of time. The gentleman conducting the interview appeared on stage and strolled up to the microphone stand. The chatter quieted down as he greeted and thanked the audience for coming. He then introduced the guest author. KJ was about to take a sip from her bottle of green tea when Gino Bartolinni appeared on stage. She froze as if someone had pressed a pause button. She regrouped from the shock of seeing Mr. Eye Candy again, lowering her bottle and recapping it. Gino noticed the beautiful lady in the yellow sundress and gave her a wink as he shook hands with the interviewer, before waving to the audience. By the reaction of the women in attendance, you could tell he was making a lot of panties wet; including KJ's.

The more KJ listened to Gino's story on how he became an author, and chose the genre of romance to write about, the more interesting he became. Besides wanting to screw his brains out, she wanted to know him on a more personal level. She crossed her legs for the umpteenth time, squeezing her thighs tightly together, trying to control the urge she was feeling in her southern hemisphere. As Gino continued with his interview, KJ began to daydream about how it would feel if Gino relieved her of the built up tension she desperately needed to release. Her eyes were affixed on Gino's crotch when he suddenly looked over at her, catching KJ off guard. Her heart skipped a beat, but she didn't look away. Gino gave her a pleasing crooked smile and turned his attention back to the interviewer. "That was awkward," KJ thought to herself as the sensation between her upper thighs become more intense. Her body won the battle over her mind, telling her she needed an orgasm now! She decided to leave the event and go handle her business. Gino glanced at her as she made her exit, admiring the way her sundress hugged her sexy curves. "I wonder what her story is. Whatever it is, I would like to get to know her," Gino thought to himself as he watched KJ leave the room.

KJ couldn't get to her room fast enough, as her thoughts of Gino had her so horny. She reached inside her shoulder strap purse, retrieved the plastic room key, and inserted it in the slot device on the door. Once inside the room, she quickly stripped off her sundress. She reached inside her suitcase and pulled out a black velvet pouch, containing her expensive dildo. She took her 'For the Moment Man' from the pouch, turned it on, and began to massage her clit as she walked over to the bed. She removed her thong and was comfortably positioned on the bed as she slowly inserted her imaginary man deep inside her love canal, moving it in and out as her soft moans filled the room.

*****

A few hours later, she woke up rested and a little less stressed. With the curtains still open, she looked toward the window and saw it was dark outside. "Damn! I sexed myself into a deep sleep," she said in a whisper, getting out the bed walking toward the bathroom to take a shower.

An hour later, dressed and refreshed, she had a taste for some Sushi. Checking her iPhone, KJ found a restaurant called Sushi Roku, not far from the hotel, and decided to take the short drive there to check it out.

When KJ walked into the restaurant, she immediately noticed Gino sitting alone in a booth. She was going to act like she didn't see him while being escorted to her table by the restaurant hostess.

"Well, hello!" Gino blurted out with a smile, stopping KJ in her tracks.

"Hello, Mr. Famous Author. How are you? KJ asked momentarily, stopping the hostess who was showing her to her table.

"Would you like to join me? I'm all by myself and would enjoy the company." KJ looked at the hostess, letting her know she would sit at the table with Gino.

The hostess placed a menu in front of KJ and asked them both, "What would you like to drink?"

"I'll have a 'Passion & Spice' (Absolut Vodka, Orange Curacao, Crushed Jalapenos, Orange Slices, Lemon Juice), and a glass of water with a lemon wedge." KJ ordered, closing the menu.

"I'll have a 'Salary Man' (Dewar's 12, Scotch, Daiginjo Sake, Sour Raspberry-Cilantro Mash), with a glass of lemon water as well." Gino said with a smile.

"Okay, I'll give you a few minutes to look over the menu while I get your drinks. Your server will be here shortly to take your orders." The hostess smiled as she walked away.

"Not trying to be too forward, but that dress looks lovely on you."

"Nothing forward about that," they both laughed at her reply. "Thank you for the compliment."

"You're welcome. One thing I'd love to know."

"What's that?"

"What is your name, lovely lady?"

"My name is Kehli Joyce but my friends call me KJ," she replied with a sensuous smile.

Absorption Vegas

"It's a pleasure to finally meet you Ms. Kehli Joyce. Another thing, you need to stop following me. Are you cop?" He asked jokingly, but trying to look serious.

"Since I was walking by and you stopped me, you might want to take your own advice. To answer your other question, no I'm not a cop but I am a LAPD Detective," she replied with a slight grin.

"That's very interesting. A detective that is as beautiful as you are, I have to put you in one of my books."

"If you do that, you better make her very interesting." They both laughed at the comment. The flirting was in full effect between the two of them. Their chemistry seemed to be connecting in a way they both secretly hoped it would.

"Good evening. My name is Henry and I'll be your server. Have you made up your mind about what you want to order or do you need a little more time?" The young man asked, with a slight smile dividing his attention between Gino and KJ, but focusing more on KJ because her beauty was captivating.

"We're ready to order. For the appetizer, we would like the Fried Calamari and I'll have the Tako Roll (Spicy Octopus topped with Spicy Tuna)," KJ ordered, handing her menu back to the server.

"I'll have Shima Roll (Shrimp wrapped with Spicy Tuna)," Gino rounded out the order; handing the server back the menu. The young man walked away and Gino turned his attention to KJ. Not saying a word, he just looked at her with a slight smile.

KJ reached into her purse, pulled out a nickel and placed it on the table. "You can write some of the best romance books on the market, but you're just going to sit there and look at me? Here's a nickel. Now, share your thoughts," she said, sliding the coin closer to him. Gino laughed causing KJ to do the same.

"Kehli, looking like you look, don't ask me that."

"Why not? I paid you good money to hear it."

"Then, I'll be forced to tell you."

"And..?"

"And what I want isn't on this menu."

Enjoying the verbal sparring she laughed and replied, "Likewise, but for now we'll stick with what we ordered."

While enjoying their dinner, conversation, and drinks, lingering in the back of KJ's mind was the thought that she wanted to do something she hadn't done before; screw this man after their unexpected, unofficial first dinner date. She had never been into the one night stand thing. But, the more time she spent with him, the more she leaned towards doing just that.

A couple of hours later, they left the restaurant and KJ offered to give Gino a ride back to the hotel, since he had walked there.

"Damn, the cologne he's wearing smells so good. It's got me so moist. It would be a miracle if my panties aren't sopping wet," she thought to herself. He walked with her to the driver's door and opened it for her.

"Thank you, handsome. You are a true gentleman," she said, unintentionally brushing her breast against his arm while getting into the car. He closed the door, before getting in on the passenger side.

"What is the name of the cologne you are wearing?"

"It's called Versace Eros. You like it?"

"Yes, it smells nice." She replied, placing her hand on his lap as a friendly touch. Instead of feeling his thigh, she felt a third leg that was very hard. She momentarily froze, surprised to find him in that state. She looked at Gino and he looked at her. Instead of moving her hand away, KJ began to massage him. Her panties were now soaked as they leaned in toward one another, kissing passionately. After a couple of minutes of tongue dancing, they broke apart from the kiss.

"Mmmm, that was very nice," Gino said as he licked his lips, staring at her lips.

"I agree," KJ said, before gently biting her bottom lip. "The night is still young. Let's go to that club I hear so much about, at the MGM."

"You're talking about Studio 54."

"Yeah, that's it!" KJ responded with enthusiasm. "Let's park the car and take a cab so we can get our drink on and not worry about getting a DUI. The last thing I want to do is go on vacation and get a DUI, giving my job ammo to fire me."

"I understand, Ms. Officer," Gino replied.

*****

Inside the MGM Grand, they waited in line to get into Studio 54. Moving through the crowd, holding hands, so they wouldn't get separated. Finally spotting a corner that they could carve a niche out of for themselves, they quickly occupied the space. Standing so close they could almost draw in each other's breath, they looked into one another's face and began to smile.

"Close quarters, huh?"

"Yes, very close. Is that a problem?" She asked, sensually biting down on her bottom lip.

Gino grinned, "Not for me. I actually like it."

"I bet you do," she replied, placing her hand on his chest and abs.

"Would you like something to drink?" He asked looking at her full lips.

"Thanks, not right now."

"I guess that means you want to work up a thirst, first."

"Yeah. Let's dance because we didn't come her to hold up the wall."

Blazing another trail through the mass of partygoers, they got a piece of real estate on the crowded dance floor. Gino had been watching her sexy figure all night in that black, body hugging dress. As she started dancing, he was mesmerized as he watched her move to the music. It was a thing of beauty. He imagined her taking off that dress and replacing it with him.

KJ also noticed how smooth Gino moved to the music. Instinctively, she knew without a doubt that a man who could move like that could rock a woman's world in the bedroom. About an hour and half, and two drinks later, they were ready to leave the club.

Getting into one of the many taxis lined up outside, they told the taxi driver their desired destination. As they settled in the backseat of the taxi, KJ gave in to what she'd been thinking all night.

"I want you. I need you," she whispered in Gino's ear. Gliding her hands along his shoulders, chest, and torso, moving her hands down further to the area around his zipper. She gingerly moved her index finger across his lips and looked him in the eyes and said, "Your body is my party." He leaned toward her and kissed her with intensity. The kiss was so intense, she forgot for a moment that she was in the back of a taxi. She couldn't remember the last time a man had kissed her the way he did, invading her soul.

"Venetian!" The taxi driver announced for the second time. Regretfully, they pulled their bodies apart. KJ was smoothing her hair back and pulling her dress down, while Gino adjusted himself in his slacks. After paying the driver, they walked into the hotel lobby showing no public display of affection. Their conversation was about his writings and the events that were going on around town.

Getting into the semi crowded elevator, the conversation between the two was silent, but their minds had them screwing each other's brains out.

"Excuse me." KJ said, to one of the occupants in the elevator as she reached to press the button for the 17th floor. The ride seemed like it was taking forever. Once the elevator doors opened it felt like they were speed walking, but in actuality they were walking at a normal pace. The door to the room wasn't all the way closed before they were all over each other; kissing, fondling, and pulling off each other's clothes. Their lust, passion, and desire to explore one another's body and to fulfill their wants and needs, were in full effect. Shoes were flying, clothes were almost torn off, and the heat of them coming together threatened to incinerate them both.

Gino was kissing her senseless again, as she moaned. His lips attached to the twins and he fed, hungrily.

The tingling sensation was sending her over the edge. She was so wet she wanted to scream, "Now Gino, now!' But she was a greedy girl and wanted as much stimulation as she could get, for as long as she could get it. So she paced herself to enjoy his mouth and tongue on her breasts a little bit longer. His magic tongue slithered down her firm, but soft body until he landed between her moist thighs. She let out a scream of pure animal delight as he found her pink pearl and twirled his tongue around it with bursts of light short suctions. KJ began to buck as if she was on a horse at a rodeo. She held onto his head and came so hard she felt dizzy, as if she had been spun around. They momentarily separated; KJ looking into his eyes, reading his intent. He stood up, lifting her at the same time, slamming his hardness into her repeatedly, while walking towards the bed.

Easing her off his erect penis, he laid her down on the king sized bed. KJ not wanting to let go, held onto Gino with lustful eyes. He placed her legs over his shoulders, guiding his steel hard shaft in her wet, tight vagina. She let out a loud moan of passion as his inches disappeared inside her.

A few short minutes into their lovemaking, KJ had an intense orgasm like never before. It had been awhile since she had been with a man, enjoying a sexual experience. She was in such a euphoric state that her reality was feeling like a fantasy.

The rhythm of his strokes had her hornier than ever. KJ began thrusting her hips upward; matching Gino's stroke for stroke, trying to get him to release his liquid of life into her.

Her attempt backfired as she screamed out, "Shiiit! Shiiit! Baaby! Ahhh!" Having another intense orgasm, she gently bit down on his shoulder, as her body shook uncontrollably. What seemed like minutes, but was only seconds; she managed to say through heavy breathing. "I'm tapping out. I want you to come now." Breathing heavily himself, Gino replied.

"Okay honey, turn around." He instructed KJ, as he positioned her on her knees and she took ahold of one of the pillows on the bed; hugging it like a plush bear. With her head down and booty in the air, Gino gently slapped her on each butt cheek before entering her. Holding onto her hips and enjoying the sight of her firm, shapely ass, he went to work.

"Oh yeah, fuck me! You want this? Show me how bad you want this pussy," she spoke through clinched teeth. She placed her left hand between her legs, also wanting to feel him going in and out of her special place. Moving her hand to massage her clit, she immediately began to squirt.

"Aww shit!" Gino blurted out, indicating he was about to come.

KJ buried her face into the plush pillows, letting out screams, as she squirted intensely. At that very moment Gino shoved deep, into her releasing intensely. He collapsed onto her back, with his now semi hard shaft still inside her. Their hands clasped together, sweating and breathing hard, they began to chuckle.

"That was so good," she whispered. "It's been a long time since I've been with a man. I almost forgot how it felt to be held, fucked, and made love to."

"I'm glad you chose me to help bring back that feeling."

"Mmmm, so am I."

"I never thought I would be involved, and fall for a cop."

"Detective!" KJ replied jokingly, but at the same time serious about her title.

"Okay, honey. I stand corrected, Detective."

"In all fairness, I never thought I would feel the way I do about a writer; the way I feel about you. Gino, I want to ask you a question?"

"Yeah, baby. What's up?"

"I know this is soon, but what would your thoughts be in supporting the idea of me making a lateral move to Homeland Security, here in Vegas?"

"That sounds good, baby, because I'm not good with long distance relationships. Besides, I need to have your soft body right here next to me."

"I'm just a soft body? There are a lot of women here that would love to be your soft body."

"Yeah, but I know how I feel about you."

"So you're alright with the idea of me moving here and being in an exclusive relationship?"

"Yeah, baby. I'm definitely alright with that. I need a woman like you in my life, to keep me balanced. I'm ready to settle down and I want it to be with you."

For some reason, tears began to travel down KJ's cheeks. Maybe the emotional rollercoaster she was on, caught up with her. Or maybe she longed to hear that from the man she had fallen in love with, on this first date.

"What's wrong, baby?" He asked, as he wiped her tears away and kissing her on the lips softly.

"I'm happy," she replied, laying her head upon his chest.

*****

The next day, deep in thought, KJ relived her first date contemplating this new man in her life. She loved how he called her Kehli, instead of KJ. Her name sounded so good coming out of his mouth. He made her laugh, made her feel treasured, and made her feel safe.

She only felt partially alive, thanks to her close sisterly relationship with her late partner, Ramon. But feeling totally alive, she never thought would really happen. She settled for the platonic love with Ramon. When he was killed, her feeling of being alive plummeted from feeling partially alive to barely alive. KJ didn't even realize how big the hole in her heart was, until Gino began to fill it. He basically filled in for her family, which she was estranged from. Even though she knew her and Gino had just met, she instinctively felt their relationship would evolve into a long lasting one.

Chapter Six
Sea Lamprey

Outside of LAPD Headquarters, on West 1st Street, a press conference was being held in reference to the bizarre death of Senator Davis, a few weeks prior. Public Information Officer, Beth Tinker, opened by saying, "We believe the political figures are being shot with bullets made with an ingredient from the Sea Lamprey."

"What is a Sea Lamprey?" A reporter in the middle of the crowed asked.

Microbiologist Dr. Newman stepped up to the microphone and explained, "A Sea Lamprey is a jawless, primitive, eel-like creature with large reddish eyes; and a single nostril on the top of its head. It has rings of teeth that favor the creatures from the movie, Tremors. They latch onto their prey and rip out a hole with its rough tongue. Then, the sea lamprey will suck the body fluid out of the fish. A special chemical in the sea lamprey's saliva will secrete a digestive fluid that slowly eats away the host. This creature can grow up to three feet and can be found along the United States' eastern seaboard. We believe, somehow, the killer is using this creature's fluid and harnessing it in a bullet form; to use against his or her selected victims. So when the victim is shot, the bullet dissolves very quickly, leaving no trace at all."

"So are you saying this person, is using a Sea Lamprey to kill these people?" A reporter in the front asked.

"We think the type of chemical this person is using, attacks the skeletal part of the human body; disintegrating it. It's the same thing the Sea Lamprey does to other sea creatures."

"So is it safe to say that you don't know what kind of chemical it is? You are speculating that this chemical bullet is made up with the Sea Lamprey's poison."

"Yes, we are saying that at this present time."

"Do you know why these specific people are being targeted?"

"I will let Chief Seaton answer that." The doctor moved away from the podium as Chief Seaton positioned himself to speak into numerous microphones.

"We have an idea, but will not release any particulars because this is an active investigation."

"Do you have a lead on the suspect or suspects?" Another reporter asked.

"Not at this time. We are working closely with Federal and State authorities, along with other local agencies, on this matter to bring the perpetrator or perpetrators, to justice. As soon as we have anything else new, you will all be updated."

Reporters yelled out questions over one another, directed at the Chief. He ignored their questions and continued to walk away with his entourage. Ms. Tinker stopped and leaned toward the microphone on the podium, "When we have more solid information to release, we will let you know so you can help us get that information disseminated out to the general public. Thank you!" She added before walking off and catching up to the Chief.

Chapter Seven
A Few More Victims

The Ghost Killer was preparing to add more victims to the list of lives already taken. Four bullets were removed from a specially designed box. The shelf life on these bullets, once removed from their crypt, is only three minutes. The Ghost Killer attached a silencer, before loading all four bullets into a see through magazine and locking it in place on the modified sniper rifle. A bullet was chambered, ready to be sent to its target.

The Mayor of Phoenix, Mayor Quinn, was at the podium giving a speech on the city's economic situation and the cutbacks she planned on implementing to get the city back in the black; along with celebrating the lowest homicide rate in the city's history. The governor, along with two state senators, were also in attendance. Security was heavy and ready for anything that may occur, or so they thought. The Ghost Killer was about the distance of three football fields away. Glaring through the scope, eyes affixed on the crosshairs that were on the targets.

A minute and a half had passed since the bullets were loaded. The bullets would start to disintegrate in ninety seconds. The Ghost Killer's index finger was on the trigger.

The trigger was slowly being squeezed to the rear and a thumping sound was made. The first bullet traveled straight for the Mayor, striking her in the left shoulder. The second bullet was immediately chambered and fired, then the third and the forth. The Governor was struck in the right shoulder and the two state senators in their legs. It seemed like all four politicians were hit simultaneously.

The security detail scrambled to cover the politicians and see where the shots were fired from. Helicopters were crisscrossing overhead checking rooftops, trying to find any signs of the shooter. The Ghost Killer made another successful hit; four to be exact, and was gone.

*****

Press Conference

Special Agent Bryant from the FBI's Vegas field office, addressed the army of reporters, "Ghost Killer" is the name the media has dubbed the serial killer, because whomever this person is, he or she can strike at any time, hit any target, and disappear without a trace of ever being in the area."

"It seems like we have a serial killer who is targeting political figures, and now adding doctors to his list of victims. We are still trying to find out what the connections are between them and the killer. One thing we can say for sure, he or she is killing political figures and doctors, from coast to coast.

Absorption Vegas

A reporter for the BRN International News turned his back to the winding down conference and towards the camera, and told the TV audience, "As you have just heard, the only information the authorities have is the bullets that are being used to shoot the targeted doctors and political figures disintegrate shortly after entering the body. Neither surgeons, nor CSI agents, were able to retrieve these specialized absorption bullets from any of the victims. Sounds like something out of a sci-fi movie. And now back to the press conference."

"Do any of the other law enforcement agencies that you are working with have anyone of interest or any idea on who this Ghost Killer may be?"

"If I knew that, I would have passed that on to you. The victims that were shot were in Phoenix, Arizona; Houston, Texas, and Jacksonville, Florida. We still don't know why this killer is targeting these specific people. None of them had anything in common with those shot in California. All we know is, the Ghost Killer is going to slip up and that will be enough for us to put whomever it is in jail, never to see daylight again."

"Since you don't know who this Ghost Killer is, there is a great possibility that many more people will be murdered," one of the reporters said with a nervous pitch in her voice.

"I wouldn't say that."

"Okay, you wouldn't say that, but who will? Because in Phoenix, the Ghost Killer managed to shoot the mayor, governor, and two state senators. In spite of the massive security detail that was in place, the Ghost Killer still got away without a trace." The FBI spokesmen didn't say a word.

"Special Agent Bryant," another reporter shouted out to get his attention. "This person kills, at will, any politician or doctor he or she desires. Even the F.B.I. profilers can't put a finger on this person's gender or race. Do you fear the Ghost Killer will never get caught?" The question by the reporter momentarily stunned the special agent before he answered.

"The Ghost Killer is a serial killer who will be caught. He or she, will do what all serial killers do; and that is make a mistake. When that mistake happens, we will clamp down on that mad dog and bring them to justice."

A female reporter in the rear stood up to be seen before blurting out, "Do you have any kind of information connecting the victims?"

"As I said before, of course we're working on finding a commonality, a connection between not only the victims but also the killer."

"With all the manpower and cooperation of the various law enforcement agencies working this case, and the high profile victims involved, is it safe to say that a doctor and/or politician had something to do with personally setting this killer off?" Another reporter asked with an intense concerned expression on his face.

"That is a possibility. Due to the geographical locations of the victims that span across the country, it's going to take some doing to sort this out and put a finger on this person. Like I said earlier, we are looking for that one mistake, that one clue, and when we find it, whomever this person is will be taken down with a quickness."

The on-the-scene reporter turned to the camera and said, "There you have it. As soon as more information develops, we will get it to you. Back to you in the studio."

Chapter Eight
Orgasms

"Hey, KJ. How are you enjoying your vacation?"

"I'm having a great time. I'm glad I came to Vegas."

"What! Am I hearing right? Is this the same woman who was ordered to take this vacation and left L.A. kicking and screaming?"

"Shut up!" KJ responded with a giggle. "So how things are back at the office?"

"It's been a little crazy with the Ghost Killer killing politicians and doctors all over the country. Be careful out there, KJ."

"You know I am. Besides, he or she isn't killing cops."

"For now, the Ghost Killer isn't. But who's to say what that person's mind frame will be in the future? Just be vigilant," Diane said with concern.

"Girl, I'll be alright. Besides, they call this person the Ghost Killer for a reason. I would never see it coming, no matter how cautious I am. So stop worrying. I'll be back next Friday to handle some business. I have something to tell you, but it can wait until I get back."

"C'mon now, you let the cat out the bag. So you may as well tell me. Don't give me that 'What Happens in Vegas Stay in Vegas' crap. I know you met somebody and got some. That's why you are acting so C.I.A. News flash, this is not a covert operation so spill it girlfriend!"

"I'd rather tell you in person. Damn, girl!"

"Okay, I'll respect that. Just hurry your butt back here. I need my shopping partner." Both ladies laughed. "Okay, I'll talk with you later."

"Alright now with your crazy self, be safe." KJ replied, laughing as she disconnected the call.

*****

The combination of drinks, and her animalistic attraction to Gino, made her hornier than she could ever remember. The door to her suite was barely closed when they engaged in a passionate kiss. Her hand moved up and down along his crotch area, as his explored her soft, but firm butt. After what seemed like an endless make out session, KJ took him by the hand and escorted him to the couch, where he sat down and got comfortable; anxiously waiting to see what she had in store for him. Standing in front of him, she began to undress like a stripper; teasing him. Removing her bra, her breasts stood firm, nipples erect, longing to be sucked. She then turned her back towards him, placing her thumbs in the waist band of her thong. She began lowering them slowly, bending at the waist, exposing her smooth bald vagina; surrounded by nice firm ass and thighs. She slowly stood up and turned around, giving Gino a sensual look. Holding her breasts she fondled her nipples with her forefingers and thumbs. Gino reached for his crotch, adjusting his hard-on. After several minutes of watching KJ doing her thing, he was ready to take care of business.

"Get in the bed, baby," Gino told her, massaging his rock hard erection. KJ walked over to the bed. Arching her back, she crawled up to the pillows. She positioned herself, sitting up comfortably. Gino stood by the bed and began to undress. KJ gently bit down on her bottom lip as she looked at the huge bulge in his pants. With each article of clothing he discarded, KJ became hornier and hornier. Licking her lips, she continued fondling her firm breast. At the same time, she was trying to control her building orgasm by tightly squeezing her thighs together. Gino loved the effect he was having on her. When he pulled his pants down, his large erect penis bounced up at full erection. KJ had enough of the show and went into command mode.

"Bring that beautiful dick here," she spoke, reaching out to take a hold of him. Gino smiled, enjoying the gentle back and forth stroke her soft hands were delivering. He eased into bed underneath the sheet and began sucking on her nipples, while massaging her wet protruding clit. She moaned loudly with the touch of his mouth and hand. In the little bit of time that Gino touched her, she could feel an orgasm about to take over her body. He positioned himself over her, placing her legs over his shoulders as he eased inside and began to deep stroke her.

"Baby, you feel so damn good," Gino whispered in her ear.

"Oh shit baby!" KJ blurted out. She called out his name as she dug her nails into his skin. Her body quivered like a 4.0 on the richter scale, as she came like never before.

*****

Gino was sound asleep when KJ eased herself out of bed and went into the living room of her suite to have a drink and look at the evening news. After pouring a glass of Vodka, she settled on the couch and flicked through the channels until she got to CNN.

"You got to be kidding me!" She blurted out when she listened to the report of the mayor, governor, and two state senators being shot at the same event almost simultaneously. A few minutes later, Gino awakened and joined her on the couch, wearing nothing but a towel.

"Hey baby. The Ghost Killer struck again in Phoenix, killing a mayor, governor, and two state senators."

"What? How do they know it's the Ghost Killer? It could be a copycat," Gino replied, placing his arms around her and gently pulling her close to him, as they snuggled.
"The killer's M.O. is the same. The same type absorption bullets are used. Whomever this person is, must have a thing for politicians."

"I'm glad I'm not a politician," Gino injected, kissing KJ on the forehead.

"Maybe you could use this prolific serial killer as a character in one of your books," KJ said, as she looked down at Gino's crotch and began to gently stoke his bulge.

"Are you for real?" He laughed. "Donna Ramos and Brooklen Borne are all over this. I know those two have already written this person as a fictional character in one of their science fiction stories."

"Is that bulge from talking about writing or is it my touch?"

"Baby, this is from your gentle touch." Gino said, opening the towel, exposing his massive hard-on. She leaned over taking him in her soft, warm, mouth.

"Aww shit! Damn baby!" Gino moaned out loud as KJ sucked him like a tootsie roll lollipop.

Chapter Nine
Instant Kill

Fear of the Ghost Killer had doctors and politicians, from coast to coast, on mental lockdown. They feared this unknown serial killer because he could strike anytime, in any place, at will. Their fear was rightly justified.

Meantime in Washington D.C., the Republicans and their 'Tea Party' were acting worse than a child having a tantrum in the middle of a toy store because his mother said "no" to getting a toy. Their arrogance, and straight out opposition, against President Obama's healthcare program caused the shutdown of the U.S. government. Over 800,000 government workers had been furloughed. That action caused a domino effect, hurting countless families that relied on the government.

Dr. Goldstein was one of the leading brain surgeons in the country. He and his wife, who was an emergency room registered nurse, lived in a Victorian styled four bedroom home in a double gated community of an affluent part of Los Angeles. They were sitting at the table having breakfast enjoying a rare day off together. All of a sudden, the glass in the dining room shattered. The doctor and his wife jumped at the sound of the noise.

"What was that?" His wife asked, looking at him. They both got up and walked toward the dining room with caution. The doorbell rang. It was the paperboy. He apologized for breaking the window because he misjudged his throw.

"I'm sorry, Dr. Goldstein. I will pay for the window."

"It's okay. Don't worry about it. Just be more careful next time," he chuckled, relieved it wasn't the Ghost Killer.

"Thank you! It won't happen again," the boy said, as he continued on his paper route. The couple stood in the doorway momentarily looking up and down the block, before descending the steps to access the damage from the outside. His wife reached down to pick up the paper that was laying on top of some broken glass.

"Honey, it's a good thing this government shut down isn't affecting us," she said to her husband, as she looked at the headlines that read: *Day 3 and Still No Resolution in Sight.*

"Thank goodness for that," he replied. As the two strolled back toward the front door, Mrs. Goldstein let out a yelp, just before she grabbed her throat with both hands and fell to the ground.

"Honey! Honey!" the doctor repeatedly called out as he held her, trying to find out what was wrong. When he saw the blood seeping through her fingers, he yelled out.

"Help! Someone, help me! Call 9-1-1" Unbeknownst to him, she was already dead. Before anyone could come to the doctor's aid, he was shot in the right shoulder, causing him to fall forward onto his wife.

Absorption Vegas

*****

KJ's day was already in full affect. She worked out at the hotel's gym, showered, ate breakfast, and was watching the local news. She was sipping on a cup of coffee, when the news anchor said, "We have breaking news coming in from California." The station then flashed to a reporter in the Los Angeles suburbs.

"Around 5 a.m., this morning, Dr. Goldstein and his wife were shot outside their home in Santa Monica, California. Law enforcement authorities say the couple came out of their home to investigate their broken window when Mrs. Goldstein, who is a registered nurse at Mercy Medical Center, was shot in the throat. The bullet severed her spinal cord, killing her instantly. When the doctor turned to attend to his wife, he too was shot in the right shoulder with an 'absorption' bullet. As soon as I get more information, I will give you an update. This is Orlena Anderson, reporting live from Los Angeles."

Chapter Ten
Homeland Security

"I'm Monique Cruz reporting live from Caesar's Palace. Ladies and gentlemen, I must tell you, if you are in Las Vegas or coming here this week, and are a fan of the literary arts, this is the place to be. This week authors, publishers, and screenwriters will descend onto Caesar's Palace for the 11th Annual 'For the Love of Books'; hosted by Ramos Barrington Entertainment. The list of authors that will be in attendance is like a Hollywood's "A" list movie premier. It's the who's who in the literary world. Check out some of the authors that will be attending: Donna Michele Ramos, Anthony Pathfinder, Dena Tyson, Beverly Rowley, Zuzu Alexi Cupido, Katrina Gurl, Brooklen Borne, Trice Hickman, Elva Nelson Hayes and The1Essence. Along with Las Vegas' own, Mr. Gino Bartolinni and a host of other favorites.

Gino Bartolinni has written several bestselling romance and suspense novels that are now in movie production. This year's theme for the events will be in honor of Trayvon Martin's mother, Sybrina Fulton, who is trying to change the 'Stand Your Ground' law. All those in attendance will be wearing black hoodies, black jeans, and black shoes to show their continued support for that family."

"Monique, can you tell us what kind of activities or parties will be going on there?" One of the news anchors in the studio asked.

"They are having all kinds of workshops in regards to publishing, protecting your manuscript, pitching your book to television and movie executives, how to write query letters and selling your book as an indie author. As far as the parties, there are so many, it's almost like a Mardi Gras atmosphere here." A passerby handed Monique an unopened bottle of beer. "See, I told you so." The news crew back at the studio begin to chuckle. "I will have an update for you at 10." Now back at the studio of WKLVA, the news anchor and co-anchor are all smiles from Monique Cruz's report.

"It looks like Monique is having a great time with this assignment." One news anchor, gleefully said.

"She sure is," the co-anchor chimed in. Looking into the camera the anchor added. "Also at the same hotel, the 'Blue Velvet Banquet will be going on."

"Oh goodness, that sounds like a security nightmare." The co-anchor chimed in again. "Well that's it folks, we will see you tonight at 10. Stay tuned for World News Tonight."

*****

Relaxing on a leather chaise, drinking from a 12oz can of Pepsi; the 'Ghost Killer' is enjoying an episode of Person of Interest. During a commercial break an upcoming segment of the 10 p.m. local news came on. The ten second segment showed a portion of the upcoming 'Blue Velvet Banquet' event that is going to be held at Caesar's Palace.

Thirty minutes later the news was on and the killer watched intensely the report on the 'Blue Velvet Banquet' event. The killer couldn't believe the event was being held at the same hotel, at the same time, on the same day as the "For the Love of Books" literary event. The killer watched and listened in amazement, as the opportunity to unleash hatred, on a scale never seen before in Sin City, on so many doctors and politicians in one place; was a dream come true. Chuckling the killer watched the rest of the report.

*****

Department of Homeland Security (Las Vegas Bureau)

While the agents were about to go over details about security for the Blue Velvet event, the 'Ghost Killer' was already one step ahead of them; putting a plan into motion.

A detective leaned across his desk to say to his partner, "This idea is crazy, to have the Literary Awards and the Blue Velvet Banquet at the same time, and at the same hotel. That is a security nightmare. Didn't they learn anything from the previous shootings? They don't know who the Ghost Killer is. He or she has free movement to kill at will, not to mention the chaos it would be if the

Ghost Killer did strike. People will be trampled to death trying to get the hell out that ballroom."

"Only a fool would allow this to take place." The other detective replied. He continued, "Hell, this is giving the serial killer a gourmet meal of doctor's and politicians on a silver platter; with a bottle of the finest wine to wash his meal down."

The captain walked out his office into the room filled with Clark County detectives, at their desks hard at work.

"Listen up! All leave has been cancelled until further notice. The Velvet Banquet is a go and all law enforcement departments in the city will rotate details for the event! The acting governor said, they will not be intimidated into not having the event."

"Well there's your fool," one detective whispered to the other. They both laughed, as they listened to the captain inform them about the command post and the perimeter their department was assigned to.

"Make sure your cell phone is on vibrate. I don't want to be interrupted by your cell ringing. Okay ladies and gentlemen this is going to be the largest security force this city has ever seen. There will be over a thousand local, state, and federal law enforcement personnel, supplying protection for this event. There will be a full briefing tomorrow at 9 a.m. sharp, at the Civic Auditorium. Make sure those of you that are assigned to this task force, rest up tonight. It's going to be a long day tomorrow, followed by long rehearsals, followed by a long day and night of protecting these people; in case the 'Ghost Killer" drops by for a visit. Are there any questions?" The captain asked looking over the crowded office.

"Yes sir!" An officer raised his hand. "When will we know if we are assigned to this detail?" The captain looked down at his watch and replied.

"In about ten seconds, those of you assigned, cell phones will begin to vibrate." At that moment, cells began to chime and vibrate. "If your phone made some type of noise, indicating you have a message, then you are assigned. Did I answer your question?"

"Yes sir!" No one else in the room said a word; they were busy looking at their phones, as they read their text messages.

"Alright then, tomorrow 9 a.m. sharp, at the Civic Center." With those words, the captain departed the area. The room became noisy with chatter; as officers and detectives talked about their text messages.

Chapter Eleven
The Day Before

The Ghost Killer had sealed a place in history as one of the most feared serial killers of all times, but the Ghost Killer was not finished. A masterpiece was about to be painted and the *Blue Velvet Banquet* event would be the blank canvas.

The Ghost Killer was sitting on the couch, thinking deeply about the Blue Velvet event. Knowing if this idea was planned right, the chance of being exposed, caught, or even killed, would be a high possibility. Feeling the buildup of anxiety, a slight smile appeared on the killer's face; indicating, this is a chance worth taking.

The Ghost Killer pulled out a wooden military style trunk from the closet and retrieved a set of blueprints of the building, where the Blue Velvet Banquet was being held. After spreading the prints out on a table and studying it intensely, the killer started placing symbols on various parts of the prints. Once finished a smile again appeared on the killer's face.

*****

Gino emerged from the bathroom naked, drying himself off from a refreshing shower, when there was a knock at the door. His cell began to ring as he walked toward the door to see who it was. Answering the phone, he looked through the peephole. It was his friend and fellow author, Jaylen, on the phone and KJ at the door. Opening the door, she walked in and immediately bit down on her bottom lip, loving the sight of the sexy picture that stood before her.

"Hey J, what's up?" He answered the phone, while giving KJ a soft kiss on the lips.

"Yo brother, I have some major after parties lined up for us to go to."

"That sounds good to me," Gino replied, but his eyes were glued on KJ, knowing her time was very important. Even though she was on vacation, no one was going to share her special moment with Gino. Not even the person on the phone.

She walked up to him and removed his towel, leaving him fully exposed. She then walked over to the bed, placing her purse on the table. She slowly unbuttoned her blouse removing it and her bra. Her firm round breasts and hardened nipples were calling for Gino to pay them some attention. Jaylen, was steady talking, but Gino wasn't answering back. He was vaguely aware that his friend was still on the line as he looked at KJ's sexy semi-nude body.

"Gino! Yo man, are you alright?"
"Yeah bro, I'm good. I have to go. I'll catch up with you at the event," Gino disconnected the call before Jaylen could even respond, never taking his eyes off of KJ.

Enjoying the effect she had on Gino, she removed her heels, unsnapped her jeans, and lowered the zipper. He was now fully erect and hornier than three people. KJ turned her back to him, bending at the waist as she lowered her jeans and thong at the same time, exposing her delicious looking vagina. From where he was standing, he could see how wet she was. She got on the edge of the bed facing away from him on her hands and knees, with her back arched; just before hugging one of the many pillows. Gino couldn't take it anymore. Quickly walking over to her, he gently massaged her pink velvet, before bending down to give her a nice slow lick.

"Oh, damn baby. That feels good," she moaned, looking back at him. He raised up, taking a hold of his joy stick and guided it inside of her. Holding onto her waist, he began to feverishly give it to KJ with no mercy; just the way she liked it. Even though her head was buried in the pillow, her moans and screams still filled the suite.

"Yes! Yes! Oh God yes, baby. Fuck me!" Her muffled vocals did not drown out the sound of Gino's thighs slapping against her behind as he penetrated her deeply. She was in such a euphoric state that she lost count of how many times she came.

"Is this good to you, baby?" He asked breathing hard.

"You know it is, daddy," she moaned.

He continued to drive his stiffness deep and hard inside of her. KJ grasped at the sheets as she came again and again, covering Gino's hardness with her sweet nectar as some dripped onto the sheets. His rhythm started to quicken. That was an indicator he was about to come. Pushing her ass back to meet his thrust, Gino came hard;

grunting loudly. Her pink velvet had such a grip on his hardness that when Gino pulled out, his condom came off and was dangling at her entrance.

KJ reached between her legs and removed the condom and tossed it on the floor; before moving to the middle of the bed. Gino still breathing heavily crawled into the bed next to her. After a short nap, they both awoke in a loving, cuddling position. KJ took her index finger and gently glided it along Gino lips.

"I must really be feeling you because I let my walls down with you."

"I'm feeling you too, baby. No matter what KJ, we will always be connected," he spoke softly, just before kissing her on the lips. KJ smiled and snuggled closer to him.

"So, have you made up your mind about moving here?"

"I'll tell you after the event. But right now let me catch myself; because you put it on me real good daddy."

"That's my job, to totally satisfy you." Gino laughed, kissing her on the top of the head and hugged her firmly in the spoon position.

Chapter Twelve
Blue Velvet Banquet

The day of the event...

Federal, state, and local law enforcement agencies had uniform and plainclothes officers inside and outside the event; along the perimeter, covering a five mile radius surrounding *Caesars Palace*.

"I can't believe they have all these renowned doctors and politicians at this event, with a serial killer on the loose targeting those in their profession," one agent of the task force said to another.

"This person is called the Ghost Killer for a reason," the other replied.

"Stay off the air, gentlemen, and be vigilant," the Operations Leader warned the security detail. He then did a roll call, while walking the inner and outer perimeters. They all reported no unusual activity.

Two hours into the event, as awards were being presented and recognition given to the many achievements in their specified field of medicine, all hell broke loose.

There was a loud explosion on the roof of the hotel. At the same time, flash bang grenades went off inside the banquet room, causing a deafening sound and temporary blindness. Everyone was holding their ears, as some people fell to the floor screaming. The plate glass window shattered and the sounds of terrified guests spilled out into the streets. Screams became intensified as people yelled out from feeling sharp, hot pain hitting them in the shoulders, legs, thighs, arms, and buttocks.

"The suspect is in the room," one of the snipers spoke into his mic.

"Contain that room now! Do not let that damn killer escape!" The Operation Leader commanded. "Do we have a visual of the suspect?" He asked.

"Team 1?"
"Negative."

"Team 2?"
"Negative."

"Bird Eyes?"
"Negative."

"Sniper 1?"
"Negative."

"Sniper 2 and 3?"
"Negative." "Negative."

"Sniper 4?" No acknowledgement was returned. "Sniper 4!" There still was no reply. "Get a visual on Sniper 4 now! Does anyone have eyes on the killer?" The Team Leader yelled into the headsets.

"Team Leader, this is Team 1. We have a visual on Sniper 4. He's tied up; not sure if he's dead. Stand by."

"Shit! Make sure this perimeter is locked down. The Ghost Killer is among us. Do not let this person get away!" The Team Leader informed them with urgency.

"Team Leader, this is Team 1. Sniper 4 was knocked out, but he's okay."

"I want to know if anyone left the room just before the shooting began. I also want all surveillance footage from any and all cameras in a three mile radius. Whomever this person is, their target was specific. None of the security personnel were harmed. Ninety percent of the doctors and politicians in the room have been hit and are expected to die!" The Special Agent in Charge barked, as personnel in the office and on the street scrambled to get the requested information.

"With all this security, we still don't know who this damn Ghost Killer is." One of the special agents on the taske force said aloud.

"This damn Ghost Killer has caused fear of epic proportions that haven't been heard of since that damn sniper in DC." The Team Leader commented, not talking to anyone particular.

*****

Ramos & Borne

The atmosphere outside the hotel was one of pure chaos. There was panic, confusion, and smoke bellowing out of the windows. The crying and screaming, of people begging for help, continued to fill the air. The Ghost Killer had struck again, on a scale no one thought could be pulled off at this magnitude. Despite two helicopters in the air, numerous law enforcement agencies working together, with multiple SWAT units, and snipers that covered the events at the hotel; chaos had still erupted.

First responders were now heavily on the scene, attending to the mass casualties and trying to get some kind of controllable order to the situation.

Gino was outside amongst the confused crowd that had been evacuated. He was frantically looking around for KJ, and she was doing the same; looking for him.

"Gino! Gino!" KJ yelled out frantically when she saw a glimpse of him through the crowd. He turned his head in the direction from which his name had been called and saw her.

"Are you all right, baby?" He asked, kissing her on the lips.

"I'm fine honey," she replied, reassuring him. "Whomever this person is has a serious mission to kill politicians and doctors," KJ said out loud, not talking to anyone in particular as she looked around the sea of mayhem. Gino just held onto her, surveying the area as well. "If I get a chance to shoot this Ghost Killer, I'm going to do it without any hesitation," she said slightly pissed, and feeling a little uneasy without her guns.

"Take a number, baby. A lot of people are gunning for this person. But if it's you, at least he will see a beautiful, sexy detective as his last picture before his lights go out."

"The killer may be a woman."

"Well the same thing applies to her as well," KJ chuckled; as Gino adds, "C'mon, let's get out of here. I have an uncle who lives close by. At least we can get cleaned up and rest. We'll come back in the morning when this mess is all gone."

"Sounds good, except we don't have a change of clothes and you are hella dirty," she replied looking Gino up and down.

"Don't worry baby. My uncle has this new invention called a washer and dryer. It will make our clothes fresh and clean."

"That's good to know, smart-ass." They both laughed as Gino hailed a taxi.

Fifteen minutes later, they arrived at their destination. Gino paid and tipped the driver, before exiting the taxi, and walked up the driveway. The house was a beautiful single level home with a stone brick front and a desert theme landscape.

"Is your uncle expecting us? There are no lights on. I don't want to intrude."

"It's all good baby," he insured her, as he retrieved a set a keys from his pocket and inserted one of the keys into the lock. "Besides, he's not home. He's away for two weeks on business."

"Cool!" KJ replied, looking around the well-manicured landscape.

Once inside, Gino turned on the lights and told KJ to make herself at home, while he did a quick check throughout the house. She slowly walked toward the framed pictures that adorned the family room.

"Hey baby, you want anything to drink?" Gino yelled from the kitchen.

"Yes, what do you have?"

"Orange juice, water, Pepsi, Mountain Dew, and Heineken."

"I'll take a Heineken. Thank you, baby." He came into the room with two green bottles, handing one of the opened bottles to her.

"I have a washcloth and towel ready for you in the bathroom, whenever you are ready. I'll wash our clothes while we are in the shower." KJ, took a swig of beer, before handing the bottle to him.

She began to undress, stripping down butt naked, before retrieving her beer and walking towards the bathroom. Gino just locked on her firm round ass, with a boyish grin. She momentarily stopped, turned around and pointed towards the door to her left. He nodded 'yes' indicating that was the bathroom door. She gently bit down on her bottom lip with a sly smile, as she turned around and proceeded on. Gino turned up the bottle to his mouth as the contents began to disappear. He drank half the bottle before placing it on one of two coasters that was on the table. He picked up her clothes and hastily walked towards the laundry room to put their clothes in the washer before joining KJ in the shower.

*****

"That was the first time we showered together. I could get used to being washed like that," she whispered to him as they laid in bed. She drew circles on his chest with her index finger.

"I can get used to taking showers like that with you too."

She saw the outline of his hardness through the sheet and began to gently stroke him before going down and taking him into her mouth. Gino moaned loudly as he placed both of his hands on her head. After five minutes of giving him oral pleasure she mounted him. That's her favorite position because she could control the intensity of her multiple orgasms. He gently massaged her clit with his thumb, taking her to a level that made her orgasm so intense, that she was about to squirt for the first time.

"Gino, daddy, shit! I'm about to come, again. Oh GOD, I'm squirting!" She screamed out; as her body shook, just before collapsing onto his chest. He held her gently as she tried to control her rapid breathing. His hands traveled up and down her back, occasionally squeezing her butt. When he felt her body stop quivering, he thrust his hips upward, making her body quiver again; causing her to have a light orgasm. Her body was moist with perspiration and strands of hair were stuck to the side of her face; sliding off him exhausted. Gino took her by the hips, raising her butt in position for deep penetrating access. He began to pound her. The noise of his thighs slapping against her firm butt was a turn-on for him; and feeling his balls slapping against her outer walls was a turn-on for her. He went after her like a man on a serious mission. She came and squirted so much that she passed out twice, each time for about ten seconds. Feeling his pace speeding up, she knew he was about to release intensely in her. A few seconds later, he exploded and KJ wanted to climb the walls but couldn't because Gino's strong hands held her in place. They both collapsed on their sides, totally exhausted.

The next morning, with her head resting on Gino's chest, the sun slowly crept up over the horizon. KJ slowly opened her eyes, and a smile appeared on her face. It felt so good to wake up in the strong arms of her man. Not to mention, the amazing sex he put on her the night before. She raised her head slightly to get a clear view of the clock on the dresser. She gently shook Gino.

"Baby, wake up." He opened his eyes, yawning and stretching.

"Yeah baby," he answered in a groggy voice.

"I have to get back to the hotel and pack." Ignoring her statement, he rolled on top of her, kissing her breasts and sucking her nipples. "No, Gino. I have to get back." He just kept kissing her, slowly moving south. Even though her mouth was saying, *"no"* her body was saying *"come get-it!"*

"C'mon baby. I have to get back, pack, and check out." But when his mouth made contact with her swollen walls and clit, she gripped his head firmly and began to grind hard against his mouth. "Ooooo, yes! Shit! Ohhh shit! Daddy!" She screamed out as she came. That was the first time she ever came that fast. He lifted her legs over his shoulders and poured his hardness in her wet canal. As he pounded deep and rapid, she dug her nails into his shoulders, throwing her hips upward to match his intensity. A few more hard strokes and he came, calling out her name. They held each other trying to control their rapid breathing.

"Baby, thank you for that good morning loving." He said, kissing her softly on the lips. Tears began to flow from her eyes.

"Honey, what's wrong?" Gino asked, looking at her with a crinkled brow.

"I'm truly in love with you, Gino," she replied looking into his eyes intensely as if she was searching for some confirmation of her feelings.

"I'm in love with you too, honey." KJ smiled as he wiped away her tears and kissed her again on her soft lips.

"Baby, can I ask you for a favor?"

"Yes, anything honey," he answered sincerely.

"Honey can you remove your penis, so I can get up and take a shower?" Gino laughed out loud, rolling off of her. She got out of the bed fully naked and walked toward the shower. Looking at the rhythm of her butt going from left to right, Gino was hypnotized. Watching her walk, he began to chuckle.

"What's so funny?" She asked, stopping momentarily, looking back at Gino.

"From the way you are walking, I put it on you real good."

"You sure did, baby. I think you broke my yum yum." She said, cupping her vagina. Gino laughed as she chuckled. "Could you please get my clothes out the dryer, honey?

"I got you, baby."

"Thank you honey." She replied, blowing him a kiss as she continued towards the bathroom.

*****

With her bags loaded into the car, she and Gino stood next to the back of the car in a loving embrace. "I'm going to put in my papers for the open Vegas Homeland Security position."

"I would like that very much, so we can be closer together and possibly start a family." A big smile appeared on her face because she wasn't expecting to hear those words, so soon from him, but was happy she did. After a long passionate kiss, Gino walked her to the driver side and opened the door. Before getting into the car, she looked at his wrist.

"I love this tattoo. I may have to get a matching one."

"I got it in Hollywood about a year ago," he said rubbing his free hand over it.

"We have to go back to that place, so I can get one."

"That would be nice and I will pay for it."

"Awww, baby, thank you." They kissed on the lips just before KJ put the car in drive and drove away. Looking into her rearview mirror, she saw Gino still standing there watching her leave.

Chapter Thirteen
Getting Caught Up

Touching the Bluetooth button on her dash, the sound of a phone ringing became audible.

"Hello!"

"Hey Diane, this is KJ. I'm back in town and I brought you something."

Diane screamed into the receiver. "Thank you, girl. I missed my bestie. When did you get back?"

"I just got into Los Angeles. I'm coming straight to your house. I'll be there in about fifteen minutes."

"Okay, I'll have a glass of Moscato waiting for you."

"Okay, bye!"

"Bye!" As soon as KJ hung up with Diane, her cell chimed again. Looking at the caller ID she saw it was the department's shrink, Dr. Coxwell.

"Hello!" She answered in a more cheerful tone than their last meeting.

"Well hello, Detective Joyce. Sounds like that vacation did you some good."

"Yes, it was a much needed one. It turned out better than I thought it would."

"Good! That's great to hear. I called to remind you about your appointment tomorrow at 1 p.m. We need to get these sessions out the way so you can get back to what you like doing. Sitting behind the desk isn't for everyone."

"You're right! Especially me! I'll be at your office at one o'clock sharp."

"Okay, Detective Joyce. Have a great day."

"Thank you! You have a nice day as well. Bye!"

KJ was starting to feel her old self coming back, but in a new-and-improved way. She was starting to cope with Ramon's death and get a hold of her life again.

Fifteen minutes later, she arrived at her friend Diane's house.

"Girl, it's good to see you. You're looking good." Diane greeted KJ with joy and energy as KJ walked up to the door.

"It's good to see you too, girl," KJ replied, hugging Diane as she entered the house. A bottle of Moscato rested in a bucket of ice next to two wine glasses.

KJ handed Diane a large decorative bag and told her it was a gift from Vegas. Diane replied, in a high pitched voice, with gratitude. She rushed over, hugging KJ like a kid on Christmas morning dying to see what was in the bag. As she did that, KJ filled both glasses. Diane let out an orgasmic scream as see recognized the expensive gift. It was a pair of Christian Louboutin red bottom, six inch, blue suede heels.

"Thank you, KJ! Oh my God! Thanks so much!" Diane kept repeating as she hugged her shoes close to her chest.

Absorption Vegas

"Girl, sit down and let me tell you about my journey."

"I'm so waiting to hear, since I only heard from you once during your forced vacation." Diane wasn't a police officer, but she was an L.A.P.D. Dispatch Supervisor. They met three years ago when KJ came into Dispatch to run a few license plates and Diane said she would do them for her. They hit it off and had been close friends ever since. "I should have gone with you after Ramon's death. I miss him too. Besides you, he was one of the coolest detectives in the department."

"I know! I miss him something awful," KJ replied looking into space.

"Enough of this conversation, girlfriend. I feel myself getting sad," Diane said, taking a sip from her glass. "So, what happened in Vegas?"

"You know the rule, 'what happens in Vegas stays in Vegas', girl."

"You know that rule don't apply right?" KJ and Diane giggled.

"Well I met this author…"

"You're talking about one who writes books?"

"Yes, crazy."

"Is he fine? Did he knock the dust off that?" Diane said, pointing to KJ's crotch; not letting her get a word in.

"Are you going to let me tell you or what? You are so damn nasty. You know he did, girl." They both laughed taking a sip of wine.

"His name is Gino Bartolinni."

"Oh shit, the famous romance author? He is fine as hell."

"That's him! I went to one of his interviews and checked him out, then later that night I ran into him at a restaurant. He invited me to have dinner with him. The more we talked, the more I was feeling him. After dinner, on our way back to the hotel, we kissed and didn't want the night to end; so we decided to go dancing. To make a long story short, I left his room the next day." KJ placed the glass to her mouth and took a sip.

"Hold up! Wait a minute! You fucked him the first night and you call me nasty? Tell me more, with details; this time." Rolling her eyes, KJ continued.

"We had a few more drinks at the club and the way he was dancing made me hornier than two teenagers on prom night, with no supervision. He put it on me like no one ever had before. I was immediately addicted to his candy cane."

"So those sex scenes he writes in his books are for real, huh?"

"Let me tell you first hand...YES!" They both broke out in laughter, high fiving each other. "I'm looking into making a transfer to Homeland Security, in Vegas. We are talking about an exclusive relationship."

"Damn girl, you must have some serious nana to have him wanting to be exclusive with you. I'm happy for you KJ, you really deserve a good man in your life. Now spread your legs, so I can take a good look at this golden kitty."

"Girl, I'm going to arrest your ass." KJ responded, slapping at Diane's hands as she attempted to separate KJ legs.

"What about the guy you've been seeing."

"Oh girl, let me tell you about that no good dog." They talked for hours, finishing off the bottle of wine as they got updated on each other's life.

The next morning, KJ and Dr. Coxwell talked in depth about her thoughts and feelings of Ramon's death, and how she was handling the situation. When their hour was up, KJ was overwhelmed with joy when Dr. Coxwell informed her that she was going to recommend her fit for duty. KJ couldn't believe it, especially after their first encounter.

"Thank you, doctor. I appreciate that. I want to apologize for the way I acted toward you when we first met."

"That's okay. I get that a lot. It comes with the territory."

"But I shouldn't have taken my frustration out on you."

"Look, just be safe out there and call me anytime. Ok?"

"Okay." They both hugged and KJ left.

When KJ reached her car, her cell rang. By the special ring tone, she knew it was Gino and a smile appeared on her flawless face. She moved her thumb across the screen to answer.

"Hey baby. How are you?"

"I'm good, just thinking about you. I find myself missing you. I really haven't been close to anyone since my sister's death about a year ago."

"I didn't know you had a sister, honey."

"I don't talk about it much, but I will fill you in, someday, on how she passed away." There was a slight pause in the conversation. "Anyway, changing the subject. I'm getting ready to go on an east coast tour with a few other authors. So I may not be here to help you move when you are ready to make the transition to Vegas."

"That's okay, honey. I will have all that taken care of. As a matter of fact, I should know something this week about whether they approved my application, or not."

"I'm looking so forward to you being here, baby," Gino said in a bedroom tone.

"Shit Gino!"

"What's wrong, baby?"

"You're making me moist, the way you said that. You keep sounding sweet like that and I just may have an orgasm sitting in this car." They both giggled.

"Wait until I see you."

"What are you going to do? Are you going to put it on me, daddy?"

"You know I am. Okay, honey, I have to get off the phone and make these flight reservations."

"Where are you going?" KJ asked, not wanting to get off the phone with him.

"I'll be touring in Miami, D.C., Philly, and New York. I might even throw in Los Angeles, as an extra city."

"Okay, honey, be careful. I'll be calling you."

"Sounds good, sweetness. I'll call you later."

"Alright honey, bye!"

Chapter Fourteen
The Surprise

The next day when KJ returned to work, some of her co-workers welcomed her back, while other's just looked at her. She continued to her desk, sat down in her chair, and scooted closer to her desk. Looking at the folders that covered her desk, she wondered who had the audacity to litter her area like that.

She wasn't seated a good five minutes, when a giddy female detective came in with a bouquet of assorted flowers, in a clear vase, walking toward KJ.

"These were just delivered downstairs for you. They are so beautiful."

"Yes, they are. Thank you for bringing them up," KJ replied, as she took the flowers and looked at the card that was attached to a clear plastic stem. She opened the small envelope and removed the card. A smile appeared on her face when she saw the flowers were sent from Gino. Her day seems like it was going to be a lovely day, when all of a sudden a cloud came in and blocked her sunshine. The lieutenant came out of his office, looking at KJ, with no particular expression. She looked at him as if to say, 'what do you want?'

"I don't know how you did it, but Dr. Coxwell cleared you for duty; and on top of that news, Homeland Security in Vegas has approved your application."

"Well, I must be in Oz, because you came out to tell me to click my heels three times and I can leave this place. SO THERE IS A GOD!" KJ spoke in an elevated tone.

"Keep your voice down, please."

"YES, SIR!" KJ replied, still with an elevated voice. She did it to get on his nerves because she was still was pissed with him.

"If you weren't a woman, I would put my foot..." KJ cut his sentence off.

"Don't let my gender stop you, Lieutenant," she said, standing up and coming from behind her desk, walking toward him; daring him to do something. The office became silent, as the detectives in attendance looked on. He made a fist and KJ smiled, hoping he would throw the first punch. She'd been waiting a long time to go one-on-one with him.

"C'mon detective, stand down," the sergeant said, moving her away from the lieutenant.

"I'm good! I'm good!" KJ replied, walking back to her desk. The lieutenant glared at her, before he turned away to go back into his office. She stared back at him until he closed his door. She went back to her desk, gathered up her things, and left the office.

*****

Later the next day, during the evening, KJ was relaxing on the couch in her living room eating some Chinese takeout after a full day of packing up one of her three bedrooms. She was watching one of her favorite television shows, 'Person of Interest', when a news special report interrupted her program. She sucked her teeth as she got up and walked into the kitchen to pour herself a glass of Coca-Cola. Coming back into the living room, she stood by the couch sipping from her glass of soda, watching the rest of the special news report.

As she watched the news report, the glass of Coke, she was firmly holding, suddenly slipped from her hand and shattered on the floor. Not taking her eyes off her 42 inch flat screen television, she continued to stare with a horrified expression. She couldn't believe what she was hearing and seeing.

She grabbed her cell and dialed her aunt's number. The phone rang a couple of times before a message came on, sending her to voicemail. KJ flopped down onto the couch, in disbelief, as tears ran down her cheeks.

To be continued…

In
ABSORPTION Miami

Music to go with **ABSORPTION** Vegas

1. Love Connection **by** Raheem Devaughn
2. The Lazy Song **b**y Bruno Mars
3. Cold War **b**y Marshia Ambrosius
4. What I've Been Waiting For **by** Brian McKnight
5. I Care 4 U **by** Aaliyah
6. Hey Baby **by** Ashanti
7. Never Gonna Give You Up **by** Barry White
8. Love Won't Let Me Wait **b**y Major Harris
9. Body on Me **by** Nelly **ft**. Akon & Ashanti
10. Do What You Want **by** Lady Gaga
11. Heaven or Las Vegas **by** The Weeknd

www.ingramcontent.com/pod-product-compliance
Lightning Source LLC
Chambersburg PA
CBHW070500130626
46555CB00003B/1095